Pro

Dani

Copyright © 2014 by Danielle Thorne

Kindle Direct Publishing

Original Publish Date: September 2014

ISBN: 9781094695822

Copy Editor: Mary Royle

Cover Design: Blue Water Books

DEDICATION

With this seventh novel, my heartfelt gratitude goes out to all of my readers, special friends, and family who read my books and support my dreams. Without you, continuing this journey wouldn't be possible or worthwhile. I owe an enormous debt of gratitude to my beta reader for this project, Beth Lyons, and to my copy editor, Mary Royal. I wouldn't have been able to cross over from publishing houses into Indie publishing waters without your generous help. Above all, I must include my Heavenly Father and Savior for allowing me to pursue my talents and dreams.

CHAPTER ONE

Overnight, the water beneath the post-ship improved from choppy gray fists to remarkably blue and gentle rollers. On deck Julia Scott took a deep breath, relishing the crisp sea air and new day. She hoped her life had left stormy seas and foul winds behind. The future looked encouraging. Soon, she would be in Antigua surrounded by all of the warm sunshine one could ever desire. In her heart, she imagined nothing would be gloomy or cruel. The West Indies rumored of paradise.

A cluster of chatty petrels swooped through the rigging, and she smiled. Caroline's sentence seemed no punishment at all. She forced her stepmother's pinched countenance to the back of her mind as the attentive lieutenant returned to her side with undisguised concern on his face. "Miss Scott, I must ask that you return to your quarters."

"What is it?" Julia turned her face up to the gangly man not many years her senior.

"It's only a precaution."

Squinting against the dazzling sun, Julia realized every officer's glass was trained on the horizon. From his position at the con, Captain Hayward gave an order, and the deck rattled under the scurry of a hundred feet as it passed from man to man. The waters of the West Indies seethed with French and Spanish battleships and privateers. At least that is what Mrs. Williams first complained about when assigned by Caroline to accompany Julia to the West Indies. Travel for any woman was a terrible risk with the world in such turmoil.

She refused to let concern take hold. "Lieutenant," she began, but the officer had returned to the captain. They spoke in calm, low tones she could not hear. She strained her eyes to make out the approaching vessel that had captured the crew's attention. It moved across the water as if pulled by loping, wild stallions. Julia's little ship was a mere pony in comparison.

The boat teetered then tottered. Julia snatched onto the bulwark for balance. Boys raced up into the tops to pack on more sail. At the ship's exhilarating speed, she could tell they were before the wind. The long weeks at sea had taught her that much.

She caught a glimpse of red streamers in the distant sails. Her heart did a somersault, and a simultaneous drum roll from the small complement of marines in scarlet coats made her jump. The deafening trill sent the entire crew into a rabid pace. The lieutenant strode across the deck again, arms outstretched to protect her from harm. He caught up her hands instead. "Miss Scott, I insist you go below, please."

Concern crept into Julia's mind. "Are we in danger?" She searched his face for clues, but it revealed nothing.

"Return to your quarters. Now." A light sheen of perspiration glimmered across his tanned forehead. He guided her toward the ladder that led below to her compartment.

"Is it the French?" Fear clutched her belly with tight fingers.

"Below," the man said firmly.

"The red flag, Lieutenant, what does it mean?"

He eyed her, gauging her ability to contain herself, while her pulse thumped in her neck. "It means no quarter. Now return to your compartment and secure your belongings." He pushed her bodily toward the hatch. "Miss Scott," he added, before she ducked into the cool shadows, "bar yourself inside."

JULIA HURRIED THROUGH the narrow passageway and into her tiny compartment that included an uncomfortable cot, a miniscule wash basin, and a chamber pot. Only one of her trunks fit into a corner, the rest of her things were below in the ship's hull. She slowly picked up a loose pile of her sketches and shoved them inside the trunk. Why had she insisted Captain Hayward deliver her to her uncle without Mrs. Williams? The aged chaperone had fallen ill and could not finish the voyage to Antigua. She'd begged to return home, but Julia insisted she would not wait, so the kind post-captain agreed to offer her room and protection when he learned of her connections in the West Indies.

The grinding of cannons being wheeled forward and turned on their axis echoed through the ship's beams. What did no quarter mean? Her mind raced. She was the admiral's niece, his goddaughter, she should recollect such things.

No mercy. That was it. No mercy, as in...

Julia dropped heavily onto the rickety cot. Overhead and around her, the beams vibrated with activity. The cadence of the drum beat continued. An impending real battle could be moments away, yet she had not arrived at her destination. Her uncle could not protect her. Her stepmother would not. What had Caroline done, sending her to the West Indies all alone with the world at constant war?

She tried not to wring her hands, but time stood still. Caroline had sent Julia away like a naughty child. True, she had never loved her. Her cool amiability had decayed to disapproval after Papa's death, but to no longer provide a roof over her head was cruel. This was no month in the country with a doddering old aunt or a picnic with the revolting Mr. Carver. It was the Royal Navy and the wilds of the West Indies.

The ship's timbers vibrated in agreement then shuddered with such force they threw her to the rough-hewn boards at her feet. A boom of artillery pushed her ears into her head. Through the folds of her long puce pelisse, she clutched her chest. Her mind reeled as the intruders fired, and by the instantaneous sounds of the explosions, found their mark.

In long cycles that seemed too far apart in time to be prolific, the post-ship answered, firing its meager twenty guns and quaking the boards down to the waterline. It felt like the enemy answered two times to their one. The deck pitched side to side in a dizzying dance. Julia held on to the edge of her cot as if it would safeguard her from the splintering wood exploding all around the thin bulkheads of her shelter.

A sickening smack echoed through the air as the two ships momentarily made contact. Timbers cried out. Human screams rang out over the din, and her skin crawled with horror. Julia buried her face into the cot and stuck a finger in each ear. She did not expect the cacophony of what sounded like a thousand men to clatter overhead. It took her breath away.

The shouts and the stomping grew louder. Gruff, excited voices in the passageway became audible. The hatch to her refuge rattled. "This 'un's blocked," a voice cried. It was not a foreign tongue, but her own language. She froze when the hatch burst open with a violent crash. Julia stumbled back against the bulkhead.

A hulking pig of a man stumbled into the confined space. He righted himself then his beetle eyes found Julia and narrowed. "Look-it here." His jaw slackened as he examined her like he'd never seen a woman before. A rush of bodies passed behind him. She realized the cannon fire had ceased.

"Sir," she managed to say, in more of a squeak than a whisper. Tremors of consternation rattled in her chest. He was not a foreigner, but was certainly no gentleman either. She noted his soiled clothes while he grinned back with broken, sallow teeth. His hair looked matted with dark filth.

"We got us a stowaway," he leered. He looked back to whom he was conversing, but his party had continued on to the next berth. With escalating horror, Julia watched his boot slide back behind him to ease the door shut.

"My name is Miss Julia Scott," she blurted from a throat as dry as chalk. "I am a guest aboard this ship and under the protection of Captain Hayward."

The man inched closer. "Yer captain's dead," he said, then snorted and laughed. The smell of his corpse-like breath filled the space between them. Julia averted her nose. She felt the damp bulkhead against her shoulders when she pressed back into it. Her mind raced ahead for what appropriate action she should take, and when reason flooded back she opened her mouth and screamed for the lieutenant.

The grimy villain slapped his palm over her mouth and pressed his face up against her face. Julia screamed against his hand. Her tongue tasted salt, sand, and tar. The odor nearly made her retch. Then panic launched her into action, and she struggled violently to push him away to free her mouth of his nasty hand.

Memories of chasing her brother Hiram across the lawn flashed in her mind. Childhood was supposed to be a happy time, but she wasn't a child. Not anymore. Her mother was dead. Her father was dead. Her detached brother might as well be with them. She was alone and with a monster.

The brute was fiercely strong. "Shut it!" he growled. Her head snapped back against the bulkhead with a bang. Knocked almost senseless, she was scarcely aware of anything but the painful grip on her arm.

"Harris."

Her attacker froze.

"Let her go."

It was a quiet voice, hardly above a whisper, but commanding enough for everything happening to jerk to a halt. The man called Harris still gripped her arms cruelly. He turned his head, and Julia could see past him. Someone had slipped into the room unseen.

"Let. Her. Go."

Harris's chest swelled with outrage. "Who'd ye think ye be?" he snapped back. He shoved his knee into Julia's middle, pinning her to the wall. She gasped in pain, and tears pricked her eyes.

The mysterious interloper revealed a pistol hidden behind his back and aimed the barrel at Harris, who forgot about Julia in a furious fit of temper. "This one's mine, Smith. Go find yer own, or you'll run the gauntlet." The pistol did not waver. "Useless bugger."

The men locked eyes then the man called Smith smiled. It was almost friendly. Harris whipped out a small dirk from some unseen place and jumped forward, thrusting it beneath Smith's chin with a snarl. "I'm going to split you open." A flash and simultaneous explosion rang out. Blinded, Julia smothered a scream. She shrank into the corner, knees shaking violently. "Shhh!" the pistol-wielding shadow ordered. A rush of footfalls moved toward them.

She flew for the narrow hatch, clawing for freedom, but his fingers caught her wrist and jerked her back. The doorway flew open anyway. A crowd of faces peered inside. Their eyes widened in surprise at the girl standing over a body and the pool of fresh blood.

Smith waved acrid puffs of lingering gunpowder around to clear the air. He cocked his head at Harris with an insincere face of regret. "Poor bloke," he muttered. The pirates stared. "She won't need this anymore." Smith held up the pistol like he'd just discovered it. One of the new arrivals held out a hand for it as he took in the scene with suspicion. His eyes came to rest on Julia. "The captain will want to see to this," he said.

Julia balked, but Smith pushed her toward the hatch before anyone could move. She tripped over Harris, knees quaking. He looked dead, and it filled her with terror.

"The captain ain't gonna be happy you knocked off his mate," the man standing at the hatch remarked. He appraised Julia with steely eyes and a face filthier than the pirate lying motionless at her feet.

She swallowed and shook her head in denial. "It was not me. I did not—"

The man Smith laughed, a low threatening sound that cut her off. His hands pressed softly into her back and nudged her forward. "A regular little tartar," he chuckled. The rest of the pirates laughed with him. Harris was already forgotten, but not by Julia. She could not shake the awareness a dead man lay at her feet.

They dragged her topside and threw her overboard into a bobbing dinghy. From there, she was rowed over to a worn but speedy pirating vessel. She landed with an unladylike plop on the flush deck. It swirled with bodies and water and pieces of shrapnel, a nightmarish activity that came to an abrupt halt as she floundered about in her tangled layers to stand.

Her stomach lurched. It could not be possible. Pirates were frightening bedtime stories. Short of enemies to the crown, the seas were safe in the West Indies. It had been almost a hundred years since Blackbeard had lost his head. Julia put a hand to her neck and shuddered.

A man who appeared to be in command made his way through the crowd of frightening gawkers and examined her with a salacious grin. "Welcome aboard, missee. What's King George sent us today?"

Smith stepped up behind Julia and put a firm hold around the back of her neck. "I found this below," he said. There was an instant silence.

"She shot Harris," accused another man. He pointed his finger at her like she was a witch. "She shot him dead."

A murmur of surprise rippled across the deck from the fascinated onlookers. The captain's jaw twitched. Julia watched a cloud of something unfathomable pass over the leader's face. "Those eyes," he smirked, then he glared at Smith, daring him to challenge his order. "Put her in my cabin."

Without hesitation, Smith dragged her across the telltale litter of battle toward an open hatch. Her mind protested, but her legs stumbled meekly past smoking cannons all in a row. Over the bulwark, the post-ship blazed with fire, flames shooting up like orange fingers toward the sky.

Smith dragged her down the hatch and led her toward the stern of the ship. A small wrinkled man stood bent and hesitant at the entry to a large partition.

"Grimly," Smith said in a hard voice. "The captain wants this in his quarters." The elfin man brightened like a little devil, but Smith added, "I'll see to it myself." Grimly frowned and shriveled back down again. He pushed the door open with some reluctance and let them pass. Smith kicked the door shut in his face.

"Sit," he ordered.

Julia fell into a rickety chair, the only one in the squalid space. A makeshift table was covered with dirty platters and charts. Dim light glowed from a stern window and in its pillars, particles of dust hovered like insects. She wrinkled her nose at an unpleasant stench steeping in the shadows, even as her heart thumped anxiously in her chest.

Smith drew off his belt, a forlorn strip of animal hide, and pulled her arms behind her back. He tied them together at the wrists. "What is your name?" he demanded in a suspicious whisper.

"I did not kill that man. You know I did not."

Smith breathed heavily as his fingers pressed her hands together to check her bindings. What kind of man killed his own kind? She licked her dry lips.

The odd stranger moved toward the door. Softly, he said, "There is little time before sunset. I cannot protect you." His dark wild hair was tied back, a dirty, linen shirt knotted at the neck, and a burgundy sash slung over his shoulder like a bandolier. Ragged ducks were frayed at the knees. His feet were bare; long and tanned, with toes splayed wide to balance his lean silhouette.

"Your name," he hissed angrily.

Confused, Julia could only stare. She thought of the dead man in her berth. It seemed likely she would be made to suffer if the crew believed she had murdered him, even though they were murderers themselves. This lot was the lowest of the low, one breath away from hell.

"I do not need your protection," she answered in a faint whisper. She did not feel any courage, although she tried to pretend it. Her entire body trembled with trepidation. Smith made an angry noise and stomped out the door. It slammed behind her with finality.

Quiet enveloped her. Julia sat motionless with anticipation so cruel to bear she thought she would be sick. There were no ship bells or changing of the watch, just noises of movement and occasional excited conversation. The ship soon vibrated beneath her short, sturdy leather boots. She could feel the wind urging it on.

Tears seeped into the corners of her eyes, but she refused to break down. It would serve no purpose. She should have stayed with Mrs. Williams in Nassau and waited for the Admiral to send for her. To insist she take a different ship to her uncle's station and without even a maid, had been foolhardy. She would be the death of her unfortunate, stubborn decisions. Why she could not accept her fate as an orphan and marry smartly she did not know.

The ship creaked as each minute passed by slowly. Julia shifted, hot in her bindings. She had not shed her pelisse meant to protect her from the chilly Atlantic weather. The wind and the sun felt warmer here. Perspiration trickled from underneath her arms and down her sides. Her traveling gown was rumpled and dirty.

Loud, brisk footfalls slapped toward the outside hatch. Julia raised her head and fear washed over her. The captain, balding and scarred, stepped into the compartment with a whoosh of air pickled in mildew and sea salt. She could barely make out his red-brown features in the gloom. "How is our little murderess?" he wanted to know.

The sharp-eared Grimly had followed. He carried a tarnished tray laden with food. "Where's the rum?" growled his master. The captain circled Julia like he was considering whether or not to purchase her then sat on the edge of a table. Grimly dropped the food onto it and hurried out like his life depended on it.

Julia felt the captain's hands at her wrists, loosening her bindings. He swept his hand toward his dinner when her hands were free. "After you, my dear." He did not smile, but studied her with apparent interest. She remained seated, afraid to move. Her wrists felt chafed, and she rubbed them while he looked at her with lurid admiration.

"I've never seen eyes the color of Caribbean waters," he confessed. He reached out to touch her hair, and she flinched. "But you're no golden-hair beauty, are ye?" Julia lowered her eyes, thankful for once to have plain hair no brighter than a walnut. The captain picked up a drumstick and waggled it in the air. "You ain't hungry, love?"

She was hungry and parched. Julia cleared her throat and replied, "I would like some water, if it would be no trouble."

The man slapped his knee and laughed. He turned up the flame in a greasy lamp until the space glowed with unnatural cheer. From a dirty clay pitcher, he poured a drink. The cup he offered smelled sour, but she took it anyway, closing her eyes and swallowing what tasted like warm, fermented bilge water. Her stomach heaved, and she locked her jaws to keep from gagging. The captain hooted loud and coarse.

Grimly returned with a brisk knock and handed his captain a bottle. The fierce man asked, "You want some of this, eh?" Julia pressed her lips together and stared at the floor. The captain guffawed again. He motioned to his servant with a jerk of his chin. "Git out." Grimly stopped rubbing his hands together and scurried out the door like a rat.

Julia tensed. Now would be the time to reveal herself. He would be a fool to lay a hand on the goddaughter of an admiral, pirate or no. She may have been a young woman of little importance in Southampton, but at sea her connections would have some influence, surely.

He circled her once more in the dim light as the ship raced over the waves beneath their feet. She felt his moist hand slide around the back of her neck. "Sir," she began. He leaned down

and blew hot breath into her ear. She cringed. "Captain—"
There was another knock at the door.

"Oi!" screamed the master. Julia tensed, but with relief. To her surprise and clearly the captain's as well, the man called Smith slid quietly inside.

"What do you want?" snarled her captor. "Where's Grimly?"

"He's unconscious," Smith replied. The cold response stunned the captain long enough for Smith to take another step forward.

The captain dashed to the table, hands tossing up rubbish and supplies then slumped like his knees had melted out from under him. He slid down to the floor and fell backward. A dagger handle protruded from his thick chest. Stunned, Julia watched his eyes expand then retract, trying to focus overhead. In the shadows he drew a ragged breath, and a dark stain spread across his tunic.

"You." Julia forced herself to navigate the shock tumbling over the astonishment in her mind.

"Now," hissed Smith between grit teeth. He leapt over the body of the second man he may have murdered before her eyes. A small scream squeaked out as Julia threw herself to the deck. Her arms came up over her head in defense should he strike her next.

"Quickly!" There were no other sounds except his rapid breaths. Julia raised her head, dumbfounded. Smith darted over to the stern windows and threw one open to a rose and violet colored horizon. He leaned out and looked up, then jerked back inside to avoid being seen. Waiting a few more breaths he scanned the deck overhead again. He motioned to her.

Terrified, mystified, and confused, Julia looked at the gasping man bleeding over the oak planking. She wondered that it did not soak through to the deck below. Stumbling to her feet, she took a tentative step toward the open window that appeared to be the only way to freedom. A long line of knotted rope had been fastened to something overhead. It hung down against the stern like a lock of limp doll hair. Far below, it attached to a little skiff that chased after the ship. Julia backed away at Smith's meaningful stare. She shook her head violently. "I can't, I—"

Smith looked back at the wheezing captain on the cabin deck. She followed his gaze. The crew would burn her alive if Smith accused her of murder again, but it was he who was the murderer, not she.

He grabbed her by the arm and pulled her toward the window.

"No," Julia cried.

"Hush, you must," Smith hissed. "Make haste!"

"I didn't do it," Julia argued. "It wasn't me."

"Do you think it matters?" Ridicule drew his dark brows up together. "Only your sex has spared you and not for long."

Julia peered over the window ledge and down at the churning foam. "I'll... fall," she stuttered.

In reply, Smith clambered past her, took the rope with both hands, and swung himself out of the window. He held out an arm. "Come."

Julia could barely see the skiff in the rapid onset of darkness. It was murder or drowning, she realized. Her only choice was to choose the least violent death. She swung a leg tentatively over the window's edge and held a hand out for Smith.

When he reached for her, she drew back. Her chest rose and fell at a furious pace. "Why should I trust you?" she blurted. She looked over her shoulder toward the hatch separating her from the rest of the crew.

"If you want to live," Smith said, "come now." There was no mistaking the anger in his tone.

She would fall, she knew it. She imagined the cold, salty water washing over her as the ship raced away into the night. Smith's dark gaze penetrated her soul with something she could not decipher. Squeezing her eyes shut, she flung out her arms toward the dangling buccaneer.

He pulled her to him through the empty air, as her fingers scrabbled for the thick, hemp rope. Stinging bullets of sea spray spattered her legs and ankles. Down they inched, each bulky knot a milestone. Julia felt Smith waver as the sea came within meters of slurping them up. She dug her nails into the line so deep she felt them bend. Unexpectedly, the ship's motion changed course, and Julia slammed over and over into the stern as the ship rose and fell over the waves. The rope began to twist and turn from their uneven weight, and she stifled a scream. Somehow, the man with one arm free wrapped it around her waist, and managed to guide the bow of the little boat up beneath them. He let go of her and dropped quickly into it. She began to slide down the soaked line, and panic seized her. His hands grabbed her ankles and jerked her hard, down into the bottom of the skiff before she could fall into the water. She landed with a painful whack, the forward bench catching her ribs and punching them with the force of her fall.

When she managed to right herself, the only light Julia could see were lanterns blinking like stars in the growing distance. Smith had released the skiff's line and set them adrift. The pirates shrank in the expanse as the remote, dark sea swirled around them. The air felt warm and without the spread of canvas, carried a musty, heavy tang. A sliver of rising moon above provided little light and small comfort. Julia dragged herself up onto the seat and turned to face the man behind her who held oars in his hands.

He said nothing. She heard his labored breathing and realized he'd spent himself. Moving as far back as she dared, Julia dropped into a tight space between the bow and forward bench. She edged away from him as much as the limited confines would allow and waited.

CHAPTER TWO

I t may have been the sun that awakened her, or it could have been the gentle sway of the skiff over the morning sea, but more than likely, it was the intense stare from beneath the furrowed brows of the pirate who answered to Smith. Whatever snatches of dream lingered as Julia forced herself to focus, trickled away. Her back ached, and her right foot tingled madly. It had fallen asleep with her.

The sky glowed luminescent as a pearl. Around her, the water stretched for eternity in every direction. Julia peered over the side at its inky blueness, surprised upon closer examination to see the foaming bubbles sliding past them were a shocking turquoise green. The water appeared to be as vivid as she had heard, but more beautiful than she imagined. She forced away thoughts of what could possibly be lurking beneath the gentle waves and withdrew her hand from the side.

Smith's hands rested on the oars. He was slumped over, but his eyes were wide, examining her closely in the light of dawn. There were smudges beneath them; dark half-moons of fatigue barely discernable in his bronzed face. It was not a natural hue on him, Julia realized. The sun had burned him repeatedly until his flesh surrendered—dry, creased, and worn.

She crept up onto the seat and sat up tall, putting her back to him while facing the narrow point of the chipped bow. Behind her, he made another slow stroke with the oar. Besides the small splash, it was quiet. She looked overhead for birds, and saw nothing but a roofless sky. A breeze ruffled her hair. It also carried the smell of two sour, unwashed bodies. Julia tucked down fluttering locks of her hair behind her ears, smoothing them down and feeling no pins. She must have been a sight with her hair tangled and dress wadded. She felt hungry and seasick, and needed to relieve herself in the worse way.

"Do you even have a name?"

From behind her, Smith's querying voice sounded teasing. Julia's stomach lurched, but she made herself ignore it. Despite what she had seen him do, he had in a sort of a way saved her. Logic suggested he would kill her after he used her for whatever it was he needed. Whatever his intentions were she could only guess, but she was trapped with him in the middle of a bright blue sea, and there was nothing she could do about it. She cleared her throat and found her tongue so thick and dry she could hardly speak. "Miss Julia Scott." She tried to sound brave. That was all he needed to know.

From the sound of it, Smith pushed the oars again in another tired stroke.

"And you are?"

He chuckled under his breath. "John Smith."

"You don't look like a John." She glanced over her shoulder and saw him smile before she looked back around.

"I would give you my real name but then I'd have to finish you off."

Julia swallowed, and her palms prickled with sweat. She must not do anything to antagonize him. She'd already seen him do murder. "So they don't hang you?" she deduced in a halting voice.

He made an amused sound again. "Hanging is the least of my worries."

For a moment Julia almost pitied him until she remembered what he was. "Perhaps there would be leniency."

"Assuming you are returned."

She fell silent. Her heart once at rest, began to trot with anxiety. Her nerves were ragged. "Where will you take me?"

"That depends on the current. Why don't you have a go?"

Julia looked about and saw he meant the rowing. He stood up, rocking the boat and she caught her breath. Gingerly, they swapped seats, only Smith did not face forward but toward Julia, watching her every move as if she might somehow escape. She bit her lip, and with what strength she could muster pushed the oars through the water.

"Not bad."

She ignored the compliment, choosing instead to look past his head at the light reflecting on the horizon. It took her mind off her tossing stomach and him. Had he been a gentleman, a proper hero, who deserved decent conversation she would have informed him that she'd been just as skilled with Hiram's canoe on the little pond on their estate.

"How will this do any good?" She heaved her shoulders into another stroke. It was ridiculous to waste her energy rowing in the general direction of nothing.

John Smith searched the clouds as if they could help. "The sky was clear last night," he said.

Julia felt a trifle of relief, enough to make her plunge the heavy paddles into the water once more. He seemed to know where they were going. She felt the smooth wooden handle skim off the first thin layer of skin on her unprotected hands. "A lady should not to have to row her own boat," she said under her breath. She glanced over to make sure he had heard. He smiled, showing a level line of teeth that did not match his haggard appearance.

"A lady?"

Julia bristled at his response, exhaling loudly through her nose. He could not know anything about her. Not unless Caroline had sent out a proclamation to the entire world that stubborn Julia Scott would not practice her pianoforte, sewed poorly, disliked novels, and did not take tea with good company. This included the company of the esteemed Mr. Carver. She shuddered.

Smith tried to engage her in more conversation but was interrupted by a flock of birds racing low over the water. They called out as if to welcome the morning. When they passed, he wondered aloud what a lady was doing aboard a king's ship.

"It was a post-ship. I was only cargo," Julia answered hastily.

"For whom?"

She took the opportunity to rub her palms which were red and threatening to blister. "Antigua," she answered curtly. "I was on my way to Antigua before my voyage was so cruelly interrupted."

"It was not my doing, I assure you," Smith said. His voice held no hint of remorse. He leant across the space between them, and Julia reared back as if he meant to embrace her. "You may rest now," he said with a knowing grin at her nervous balk. She realized he spoke without the vulgar slang of his former cohorts.

They changed positions again and again as the sun rose higher and hotter, and a light wind did little to refresh them. Julia felt it blaze down on her exposed scalp, searing the tender white skin like a slab of pork. She was drowsy and choking with a thirst she had never known. Her tongue felt twice its size.

Without warning, Smith fell still. He didn't even breathe. She twisted around to see if he had fainted. His hands had dropped from the oars and laid useless in is lap. His eyes stared wide and blank beyond her. She turned about again to see where he looked. In the distance, a dark silhouette sat like a firm monument over the water. It was a solid thing, a large bulky round blemish in the middle of the vast sea.

Smith studied it then rubbed the stubble on his chin. He narrowed his eyes and looked Julia over as if seeing her for the first time.

"What?" she whispered in a timid voice.

"Land. The birds have led us this far, but we've some toil ahead if we're going to make it."

JULIA NEVER CONSIDERED how much work it took to get a small vessel into the shallows of a small cay until Smith forced her to work alongside of him. The sea seemed to have its own plans, but together with Smith heaving one oar and Julia paddling with the other, they were able to hit the high rollers just off the beach at a good angle and reach the shore without overturning the skiff.

After what seemed like hours, they pushed it up onto the light colored sand, overturned it to dry, then collapsed beneath the shade of a tree with enormous feathered fronds the size of carriage wheels. They both dropped into wet, ragged heaps in the shade. Before she could drift away into peaceful slumber in the grainy sand, Julia became sick, retching up nothing but bile. She sank into a pile of exhaustion certain she had no dignity left.

She dozed in and out of a wretched slumber, waking after what seemed no time at all. Forcing her eyes open, Smith's bare legs came into view. She noted he wore no stockings. It didn't matter. Not here. It couldn't. Besides, they were nice legs for a criminal. He was looking up into the tree over her head.

Julia followed his eyes. There were large, round nuts nestled in the top of the tree. They looked like monkey eggs. Julia studied them curiously.

"You've never seen a coconut tree?"

Julia nodded to herself. "Yes. I mean, no I've never actually seen one until I left England, but I recognize them now." Her voice came out low and croaky.

Smith sighed like she would be a burden.

"Where are we?"

His eyes shifted through the thin grove up to where the foliage thickened. Julia followed his gaze. After the trudge across the beach through soft, pale sand, the land grew hard packed, with a gritty layer of sandy dirt mixed with miniscule pieces of wood, leaves, pebbles, and insects. The trees were mostly palms but as the land sloped upward to the island's dark centered crest, scraggly silver trees twisted themselves around one another. Birds called in the distance, pleasant twitters and trills she'd never heard before. Julia put her hand on the trunk of the coconut tree and examined its splintery coarseness.

The small strip of island, that Smith called a cay, was a beautiful place, rugged yet soft, peaceful though waves crashed upon the shore and wind whipped through the top most tree branches.

Julia saw an overturned trunk and decided it a good place to settle. She was weak with thirst. Her limbs trembled with fatigue. A noise through the brush brought her right back to her feet. A trio of three dark men, truly native, emerged from the tropical jungle with wide, dangerous swords in their hands.

Smith jumped up as well. He had his arms over his head in a wild salute of surrender.

"*Oti*," he said in a firm, confident voice. They froze, eyed Smith, and then turned to examine Julia. Her appearance seemed to mesmerize them. She trembled in spite of herself, but remained quiet. She felt a ray of sunlight pierce the dappled shade and singe the burnt spot on her scalp. Suddenly, one of the natives laughed loudly. Julia saw teeth flash in his brown face then everything dimmed, and through a small pin hole she knew herself to fall heavily to the ground like a sack of potatoes.

Consciousness seeped back in unwelcome layers. Despite knowing she wasn't in a dream, her body felt comfortable and cool. Completely relaxed, Julia became aware of something wet on her forehead and something soft beneath her. Opening her heavy eyes, Julia found herself in a small shelter with a low lying roof. The walls twisted with sticks and dry vines. The floor was packed earth. She lay like a corpse on a bundle of wool blankets that smelled of sweet flowers mixed with the coppery scent of earth. Her mind spun in lazy circles so much she closed her eyes again, stretching her wrists and ankles to see if they were bound.

She was free. She took in a deep breath and gingerly tried to sit up. A small pot rested at her feet. Seeing no movement beyond a heavily netted entrance, she reached for it. Clean, cool water rushed into her mouth. It wasn't wet enough to satisfy her hot tongue. She drank until she felt sick and dropped back onto the blankets. Where was she? Where was John Smith?

Low murmurs of conversation outside of the little hut grew louder, and she tensed. A dark woman ducked into the hut with no warning, and Julia bolted up into the sitting position. She wore a short petticoat of faded, course linen. Her bosom was partially exposed beneath a sling of the same material, and a feathery, grass headdress sat on her silky, black crown. She grinned, teeth glowing in the dim light. "You want eat?" Her eyes were intelligent and her cheekbones sharp. Julia could not rip her gaze away from the long, exposed body. The woman waited patiently until Julia could collect herself.

"Yes, please, of course," she almost cried when her mind made sense of the words. The woman smiled and disappeared again, leaving Julia with the sound of her heart throbbing in her ears. She felt like she could be sick at any moment. Perhaps eating was not a good idea, but before she could convince herself of it the woman returned. She squatted down and held out a bowl so her patient could examine it. Julia took it into her hands. It looked relatively harmless. Fresh and dried fruit were cut up into small bites. She chose a small cube of something withered and brown, bit down on it, and rolled it slowly over her tongue. It tasted familiar, but she was not sure. Without shame, she gobbled down another bite, white and lumpy. It melted in her mouth, starchy and cool. She closed her eyes and relished every sensation of chewing real food. It had been so long.

Eating made her mouth water, and she drank more from the pot. She gulped like a starved kitten. Choking in mid-swallow, she tried to cover her mouth and salvage some poise, but she wasn't quick enough to catch the water dripping from her chin. A belch worked its way up out of her chest. She tried to swallow it back down, but it gurgled out anyway.

The woman laughed. She squatted onto the ground and pulled a long lock of hair from Julia's head. Though tangled and knotted, it was clearly a shade of brown, so different from the hair on her own head. Julia smiled when their eyes met. She put a hand on her heart. "Julia," she said. The woman grinned, showing strong square teeth tinted with age. She mumbled something back Julia didn't understand and leaned over to gaze deep into Julia's eyes. Before she could ask why her hair was wanted, a large shadow filled up the entrance to the outside.

The woman rose nimbly to her feet. "Capitan," she said. Julia's eyes widened in surprise. She did not recognize him immediately, and when she did, she averted her gaze. Smith had nary a stitch to cover himself. The spitting image of a wild savage, he wore nothing but a small cut of worn wool over his nether regions. His faded burgundy sash was tied around his flat belly. Beaded chains draped around his waist and decorated his ankles. His feet were still without shoes, and his torso and face were streaked with a violent red paint and yellow splotches. When her eyes rose to his broad chest, she met his gaze to censure him, but a laugh erupted from her mouth instead. John

Smith wore a feathered crown that made him look, well, utterly ridiculous.

"You look like a plucked chicken." *With long, naked legs.* The pirate did not seem affected by her opinion. Instead he spoke to the woman in a garbled tongue. She grinned at Julia again and strode out. "Where have you sent her? I need her here with me."

Smith raised a brow to question her demand. "She is not your servant." He frowned. "Our host would like to meet you. He thinks you're pretty."

Apprehension coursed through Julia's rested veins. She'd had enough rest to feel half human again, but another ominous situation now reared its head. "What do I—"

Smith turned on his heel and strode away. His departure allowed hot beams of sunlight back inside. Julia edged away from them into the cool shadows. She looked down at her dirty, wrinkled dress with disgust. It smelled like wet stockings. Combing her loose hair with her fingers she tried to fluff it up, but with no pins and no maid to assist her, the effort was futile. What would Caroline say about her appearance today? No ill-fitting gown or wild hair could compare to this attire.

The woman slipped back inside the shelter, bending slightly over so she could remain standing. She crooked her hand. "Come." Swallowing with trepidation, Julia climbed to her bare feet and obeyed. To distract herself from whom and what was to come, she tried to recall when she had removed her shoes and stockings.

THE PLEASANT MURMURS and faint fragrances of fire and fish moved from suspicious in Julia's mind to a colloquial scene of busy, happy island life. Except these islanders were not like her. They had skin the color of toast, and all of it was exposed. She made every effort not to stare, but besides the shameless children, the majority of young girls and women were naked except for a thatch of cloth over their loins. It appeared completely innocent.

Most of them sat around a fire pit in a manner of socializing and seemed excited to have guests. They chattered and laughed, pausing only when Julia was led to stand before their communal gathering.

John Smith reclined lazily at the elbow of a seated man raised above the crowd. He had more paint, more beads, more feathers, and a far fiercer expression than anyone else. It was clear he was the commander of this event and even more so that Smith hung on his every word. It was too much to take in. The nakedness and foreign voices overwhelmed her, even as the scent of roasting fish made her stomach grumble.

There was a burst of laughter from the children and older women. They pointed and laughed. Julia stood on display like a trifle for sale in a shop window. She maintained her composure for dignity's sake, unsure whether to trust Smith's amity with this people or make plans to save herself.

A flashback to the post-ship and explosions made her heart sink. It had only been two days, maybe three. For some reason, Smith had carried her thus far, but for what purpose. Beneath the dust and tar, he could have been a striking man if he had been a gentleman, but he was a murderer, a liar, and God knew what else.

She clasped her hands in front of her and dipped a modest curtsy to the chief-king. He had been watching her, she realized, while John Smith whispered silkily into his ear. The crowd quieted, and Smith found her gaze. "Sing," he commanded in a loud stern voice.

"What?"

"Sing." He motioned with his hand for her to proceed. "I hope you do it well," he added through grit teeth. The people waited, each round golden face beaming with smiles and expectant round eyes.

Julia forced herself to open her mouth and stammer out a few bars of *Robin Adair*. Smith's stone expression softened slightly, so she looked at the chief beside him instead. It was probably her host who held her life in his hands, and Smith was not to be trusted whether he liked her voice or not.

The few of the older women grinned at her, and Julia took heart. She continued the Scottish melody with flair. If only her stepmother could see her now, for Julia knew she could sing and according to the few who had her love and trust, she sang like a sparrow. It had not been fine enough for Caroline, but it gave Julia some measure of comfort. With eyes closed, she realized she had not sung since Mr. Carver had made his offer. Her concentration foiled, she trailed off on a terrible turn of pitch and mumbled the last few words of her song. For some silly reason her cheeks burned with embarrassment at her faltering attempt. At the least she should feel gratitude there was no pianoforte. She played poorly. The multitude began to whoop and clap their hands together and slap their bare legs. She assumed it meant they appreciated her performance.

Smith joined in the fray. He smiled to the man beside him and began to converse again but with more animation. Her performance, it appeared, had been the grand opening of a long supper party that took place around a pit in the ground with tall, frolicking flames. She was offered fruit and fish and fresh juice. She ate again, and as if it was her last meal. None of her captors seemed concerned with English manners.

Through the firelight, she kept her attention on Smith. He seemed at ease and familiar in this environment. It was like he'd never been on the powerful pirating vessel at all, but had danced like a king's fool in a loincloth all of his native days.

The children laughed and played, a pleasing distraction, but later they filed away to places unknown as the evening wore on. The warmth of the hot humid air cooled as breezes whisked up through the trees. Julia's eyes grew heavy. She struggled to stay alert and to smile and nod at the women who chatted to her in their wavy tongue as if she understood every word. The fire reduced its gay dancing to long languid laps, licking up all the stars. The distant heavenly lights peppered the tropical ceiling like sugar crystals. Julia jerked when she became aware her head had drooped. Beside her on bent knees, the savage woman who had tended to her laughed loud and throaty. She took Julia by the elbow and guided her back to the little hut on the edge of the quietening village.

Once prepared to sleep, Julia relaxed in the deep darkness of her temporary home. It seemed impossible that one year ago her father had died suddenly. It had come with no warning. He did not linger like Mama after the last baby. One morning he bussed her cheek hello, and the next, Julia found herself bidding his still form farewell. Caroline, who insisted Julia never call her Mama, died in her own way, too. Meaning that what little kindness she had ever showed Julia was buried with Mr. Scott. If the lady was motivated by compassion to introduce her to Mr. Carver, Julia could not see it. The repugnant memory of the gentleman made her lip curl. The thick and slobbery way he spoke her name made her nose wrinkle.

"Miss Scott."

There. Like that, but worse. Far worse.

"Miss Scott." This time her name was hissed the way John Smith hissed, like when he wanted to drag her out of stern windows. A sharp poke in her shoulder sent her scrambling up to her knees. Blind, she put her hands out in the darkness to push away the intruder.

"Smith! What are you doing in my room?"

He laughed. "This ain't a room. I'm sure you've had better."

Her racing heart slowed, relieved in a traitorous way to hear Smith's voice and not Mr. Carver.

"What do you want?"

"It's not what I want." Smith waited in the quiet, teasing her with silence until she demanded to know more.

"If you don't leave this instant I will scream."

"That would be awkward, Miss Scott. Our friends think we are brother and sister and would wonder why I'm bunking in your quarters."

"What is it then?" Julia's exasperation made her want to reach out and strike him, but she lacked the courage to attack a man who fired pistols and threw daggers with no remorse.

"It's not me, I'm afraid. It's our host. Chief Pierre has taken an interest in you and would like to make a trade."

"A trade for what?" Julia whispered in the dark. She feared someone would hear them, and Smith's words sounded like a warning.

"To be clear, he's offered assistance to help me reach civilized society in exchange for you."

Stunned, Julia could only turn this revelation over one thought at a time. "What does he want me for?" She did not really want to know, but ignorance would not whisk her away to the safety of Antigua.

"When I said he thought you were pretty, I was in all honesty embellishing the truth."

Julia recoiled. She glared at Smith in the dark, not because he did not find her pretty, but because she knew he was in some spiteful way, teasing her. Through the murk, she tried to focus on the shadowed details of his silhouette. She suspected he grinned from ear to ear and that his teeth looked unnatural in his festive paint.

"What ever does he want then?"

Smith's tone changed from gleeful to solemn. "He wants to eat you."

ON LIGHT FEET AND THIN slippers, she flew through moonlit woods. The path to the parish chapel was a way she knew well. Sobs swelled up inside of her like tidal waves onto the shore, but Julia refused to cry. She needed her strength to run without stopping, without fainting, and without pain. They would not look for her there, among the damp grass and low lying mist. It curled over and around the tombstones in ribbons of grief.

Her father's marker stood tall and strong just as he had in life. After her mother died, and the little baby boy with her, Mr. Scott swore to his only daughter he'd never leave her alone.

Julia stumbled the last few feet to the grave and fell onto her knees. Her breath came in tight, greedy gasps, constrained by a corset and pins. How could her stepmother do such a horrid thing? Julia was adamant she had no feelings for Mr. Carver. She did not want his estate with its smelly pigs and cows.

Papa would not have approved of a forced marriage. He liked the young men who lived in the village. He thought it a fine thing to marry for love, and to love someone near her own age, to be sure!

Julia fell over her knees face first and planted her forehead into the chilled earth. If only God had spared him a few seasons more, but life was cruel. For some reason, heaven saw fit that she must lose her father, which meant her home and all she had ever held dear. Caroline was her closest relative and only advocate in Southampton. Brother Hiram had grown distant, answering to events in London where gambling and liquor were as plentiful as anxious debutantes. There was nowhere else to go besides begging to great aunts and distant cousins. Whatever would she do?

THE ISLAND'S COOL, moonlit night took her back in time, but not far enough to make the rough stones and sharp seashells unnoticeable against her bare feet. Julia winced as she ran, reckless and without encouragement from the hillside village down to the sea. Smith led her by the elbow, and then the arm, and when she found her pace dwindling he grabbed her perspiring hand, and they continued their dash like paramours into the night.

When they reached the beach, she jerked her hand from Smith's grip. He made a beeline toward the row of beached dugouts, long and sleek. They reeked of fish. The shoreline where the natives had stowed the skiff was riddled with pebbles and nets and lines. It smelled worse than Portsmouth, she decided.

With some struggle, Smith upended the skiff and motioned for her in the dim moonlight to follow him. Julia needed no persuasion. She had followed him out of her little hut, and once in the shadows made the break for freedom. Now they would go back to the sea that had already tried to lose them.

Apprehension flowered in her chest as the little boat slapped over the surface of the water. Smith's shadow leapt in with ease, but it was a loud splashy effort for Julia. She'd shed her dress and petticoat hours before to rest, so she would now be a half-dressed castaway in nothing more than a shift. No bonnet, no shoes, not a stitch to cover her arms and legs. Smith, too, appeared to still be naked as a native. Between the both of them, there wasn't enough to properly dress a dog.

She looked back as the craft glided into dark waters with only the reflection of a moonbeam trail to guide them. Over her shoulder she spotted a glow on the distant hilltop. A fire had been rekindled. "Look, Smith," she said in the stillness. The skiff creaked as he turned toward her voice.

"They've awakened." His voice was calm, but it carried a meaning that made Julia's stomach sink. "Will they come?"

"Oh, yes, they will come."

Julia's pulse hammered in reply. Panicked tears pricked her eyes, but she forced them back and put a hand to her chest to stifle her raging heart. Fear would get her nowhere. Smith passed a primitive oar back over his head almost striking her chin.

"It's time to stroke, Miss Scott," he commanded her. "This time there will be no turns."

It could not have been an hour she was sure, before Julia prayed it would storm and make the chase impossible. God did not answer. This had been the usual response from heaven, but as time dragged, the lights and faint voices behind them in the pitch of night faded as Julia paddled the skiff through the midnight ocean determined to live another day. Her shoulders burned with pain. Perhaps, she guessed, they'd grown confused or could not find them in the darkness. Whatever the reason, despite the calm sea and twinkling stars, the savages she had at first found kind and good humored did not pursue them into the night. When she could paddle no more she let the oar drop to her soaking wet feet and rubbed her shoulders while blinking heavily.

"You can sleep," Smith said from the bow of the boat. He had stopped his stroking before her, signaling the danger over. His back was to her and barely discernable in the shadows. He appeared to be slumped over and sounded hoarse with fatigue.

"They won't find us now," Julia said with hope and though he did not dispute her hopeful declaration, he made no promises. After a time she sensed he was awake, too exhausted to sleep and like her, waiting for the promising pink glimmers of morning.

"You've rescued me again." Julia hated to interrupt the peace, "and from the most horrible of all deaths." She'd contemplated this irrefutable fact for a while and felt obligated to recognize Smith's selfless deed. It was easier in the obscure setting.

"Did I?"

She pursed her lips at his saucy reply. For a criminal he was jocular and easily entertained by his own wit. "I was trying to be complimentary," she sniffed. "I'm not excusing your... occupation."

From the bow, the fickle villain made a noise resembling half a cough or laugh or perhaps both mixed up all together. "My lady," he murmured, "I don't need your excuses. My occupation is none of your concern."

Julia straightened and raised her voice so he could hear her clearly. "I'm sure, Mr. Smith, that I should be concerned. You are on your way to hell you know."

Smith exploded into laughter, an infuriating response to a serious situation. "Only God can forgive you," Julia continued. She tried to control her voice so she did not screech or shout. "I have forgiven you, and you should be thankful. If you take me to Antigua you may even be pardoned."

"Oh, a pardon!" Smith mocked her in a sing song, high pitched voice. Then dropping back to his normal low tone he said, "I did not know you yielded such power, my lady."

Julia huffed. She sank back down into a pile of ragged fatigue and rubbed her aching shoulders again. It was good the man didn't know she was an admiral's niece. He might hold her and demand a ransom. He might not even give her back. For all she knew, he may not be a pirate, but a native who was lost to his own people. Maybe he wanted to eat her, too.

"You're right," she said in a repentant tone. "I have no connections. Only my uncle, you see."

"In Antigua," Smith reiterated, like it was all she spoke of.

"Yes." Julia took a deep breath, satisfied he did not suspect she had any value. He could not think her too low, or he might abuse her. Mr. Carver came unbidden into her mind, and she shrank away from the disgusting memory. No, Smith must not think her too low nor too high. "Do you know where we are going? Where the closest land lies from here?"

The man pushed his oar into the water again and gave another slow stroke in reply. His head tilted upward, studying the stars as if they were directions to follow. "I do not know where here is, Miss Scott. We are in the middle of the sea."

"But," she stammered, "you led me off. We ran away. I thought you had a plan." Smith laughed. It rang out loud and inappropriate in the silence of the dawn. Her fingers clinched until her nails cut into her palms. If he weren't so quick to snuff out life, she'd be angry. Instead she felt desperate. "We'll starve," she stated, as if he hadn't thought of such things. "I'll die of thirst or the sun—"

"Oh, you'll boil in the sun before the hunger kills you."

The simple observation made her fingers curl into fists again. She wanted to bang them on the side of his wobbly boat, but it would only cause her pain. Smith would probably just laugh again. She wasted precious breath even conversing with the man. Why he had preserved her life she had no idea.

"Who are you?" she grumbled. He heard her, she knew, but he did not answer.

Julia rolled back onto her tired shoulders and let her head hang over the side of the boat. She was too tired to care about horrible sea serpents anymore, even should one hop out of the water and gobble her up. It would be less terrifying than being burned at the stake and served up for dinner.

She squeezed her eyes shut and waited. Her life had descended into a nightmare. She was not locked in a tower or lost in her own mind, but trapped in an alien world with no control or escape. It felt as if Papa had died a thousand years ago, and left her in a continual downward spiral through levels of hell even Dante could not have imagined.

CHAPTER THREE

A blinding pinprick of light passed through her eyelids and poked her mind hard enough for Julia to realize she'd fallen asleep. It had been an unnatural rest, damp and hard, and again she found herself hungry and needing a chamber pot, a flowerpot, a soup bowl—anything would do. She knew from the aches on her beaten and bruised body she had not dreamed the dash to freedom the night before. It seemed distant and melodramatic now, like a silly novel Caroline would read while wasting away an afternoon. Julia cracked open a crusted eyelid and observed Smith. He faced her in the same awkward position and just inches away. The dream had happened.

His bare feet could have touched her curled legs if she stretched out, so she remained in her cramped position, cursing the pain in her muscles. She wished she had a silly novel to waste away the hours until she drowned herself. There would be no way she could endure another day of volcanic heat and the stinging sun. Smith did not know where they were or where they were going. He didn't seem to care.

Rubbing her eyes, Julia sat up gingerly so as not to awaken her companion. Asleep, he looked harmless. His face turned toward the sun, soaking in the morning beams. He had a curious spirit for so slight a person. He stood not a great deal taller than she, and was lean and slender, yet strong. She found it ironic his eyelashes were thick and dark, pretty for a man. An aristocratic nose contradicted his disheveled state. She grinned wide enough to feel her lip tear slightly. Her sore fingers patted away the blood she imagined leaked from her pitiful, rent skin.

Smith sighed heavily. She watched him to gauge whether he was awake or still slumbering. With such an air of peacefulness around them it seemed fruitless to agonize over the outcome of their foray back into the blue-green ocean. It lay vast and empty. Even the birds who had guided them to Smith's savages had disappeared.

The man twitched, moaned softly, and then raised himself to a sitting position. He opened his eyes, locking gazes with Julia. He looked haggard, possibly more than when he'd first rescued her from the pirates. His mouth grimaced like he could not decide whether or not to speak, but his thoughts became apparent when he crawled back up to a sitting position and picked up an oar like it weighed more than he could bear.

Julia could not think of anything to offer that would relieve his fatigue. She had thanked him for his role in preserving her life, but unless another land mass appeared majestically before them, they were doomed to drift forever until they met their Maker. The forlorn thoughts gave her something to say, although she knew in her heart it was ungrateful. "You should not have bothered."

He was the only company she had; perhaps it was fit he was no gentleman. She had wasted her opportunities. She'd been too fearful to stand on her own. If she had been brave enough, she may have found a better situation than being shipped to the West Indies to burden her poor uncle. It had been the draw of a paradisiacal escape and her childhood dreams of adventure that had convinced her.

Smith said nothing, but continued his slow paddling, the muscles in his back tightening and relaxing. They were smooth and taunt, strong and sure. Julia jerked her eyes away. Even though the sun lay just over the horizon, she was beginning to lose her senses. "You should have not bothered to save me. Now I will die anyway, and your heroic efforts will be for naught."

"Heroic? I thought I was going to hell." Smith's voice sounded rough, like gravel under carriage wheels.

"You could have joined your... your crew in their... revelries, but you chose to spare my life. I thanked you, and I thank you for saving me from those savages. I thought they were beautiful and kind"—Julia's stomach churned in disgust—"but I never suspected they wanted to eat me. It's so... well, it's savage that's what it is. Like a nightmarish tale from the *Bounty*.

Smith chuckled. "You are quick to believe everything you hear, aren't you, Miss Scott?"

"I—What do you mean?" Julia scrunched her brow. Why should she not?

"What else do you believe? What else do people tell you, and why are you alone in the West Indies?"

For a moment's hesitation, Julia considered that Smith already knew her name, and now he delved deeper into her situation. Why would he care? Then again, maybe if he knew her better, he might feel pity and put off anything other than kindness he held in store for her.

"Well," she began. It struck her as marvelous that someone besides Mr. Carver or a kind church widow cared enough to ask her anything at all.

"I'm not quite alone, as you know. I was on my way to Antigua. My uncle is there, and I was under the protection of Captain Hayward until I reached the island. I had a companion, but she fell ill and could not finish the journey."

"With the Royal Navy?"

Even though she could not see him, Julia imagined her unusual mode of transportation had aroused Smith's curiosity.

"He has... connections, you see."

"No," Smith said, "I do not. He is a councilman, I suspect? He owns a plantation or something of that sort?"

"No," Julia returned quickly. She did not want Smith to think she was titled or wealthy. Yet she did not want him to think her a pauper. Somewhere in-between must do. Caroline had often reminded her that without a large fortune or great beauty, Julia was in fact a waste and should marry as quickly as possible. A Season in London would be a sham for she could not compare with either beauty or talent for that matter. At least that's what Caroline had said, and she'd believed it. "My uncle," Julia continued, struck with sadness that she had so little to recommend her without acknowledging the admiral, "well, he is a sailor, too."

Smith made a *harrumph* noise. He didn't ask any more questions. The quiet between them felt pleasant for a time, but soon the sun rose and nothing felt comfortable at all. The unrelenting heat of midday seared through her fingers and burned her scalp. Fingers, hands, nor even the wild pile of unkempt hair on her head could shield it from the pain. Her forearms had flushed pink to rose and soon would be scarlet. There was no shade and no mercy for their lost souls.

Even in her unbearable condition, Julia knew it to be worse for her companion. He was almost naked under the sun. His broad, brown shoulders turned darker in the bright beams. Sweat glistened on his back as he slapped the oars into the water, time and time again. Occasionally he would splash himself with water and shower Julia with sea spray too, but the wetness only made her thirsty, so thirsty she wanted to lick up every drop up in the bottom of the skiff.

Tiny tears of frustration began to build up in her eyes, and where they came from she did not know. There didn't seem to be any moisture left in her body. Slow, sluggish, and yet alert enough to be miserable, she caught one on the tip of her finger. A sob surged upward in her chest, and she could no longer hold it down.

Smith turned about woozily eyeing her as if she'd gone mad at last. Another cry escaped from her cramping throat. It reminded her how thirsty she felt. Faster and faster, she began to cry until it was uncontrollable. Even as it wracked her with sniffles and moans, it felt like a cleansing, an unavoidable exhumation of all her pain and fear after being tossed out of her home and frightened near to death by pirates and savages.

"I want to go home," she cried. "I don't have a home. I have no home." Her weeping faded to choking grief. "I don't have anybody, anybody at all. I'm going to die." She put her hands over her face as Caroline's words echoed in her ears. "What a waste I am!"

She was not aware that Smith had slowly made his way across the small space separating them. He took her hands and pulled them into his lap. Long, strong arms encircled her, and she collapsed onto his leg, his bare leg, and did not care. What did it matter? They were going to die, and in their last moments he would shield her from the sun and give her somewhere soft to lay her head.

Somewhere in the back of her mind, she imagined Caroline's look of horror. Why was it not a horror to promise a young woman to a man three times her age, but scandalous to faint into the arms of a naked pirate at sea?

"Little one," said a soft voice when her outburst faded. She could not fathom why he would show her kindness now, when she wanted to slip away and be done with it. She wished she did not know it was John Smith, or know that the boat and the water and the sun were real, too.

"We are not lost, you see. This is the shipping lane to Antigua, and we will be found soon. Miss Scott?"

Julia kept her eyes closed and tried to disappear. There was no reason to believe a ship or a cay would come to their rescue. Her life did not have happy endings. It had been one tragedy after another, and this would be her last fight.

"See, just over the horizon, my dear. We've been paddling with the wind, and they're almost near. They'll see us shortly."

His soft whispering words came with a sudden cooling breeze. It lapped over the side of the skiff and across her back, rocking the little boat like a cradle.

THE LAST THING JULIA recalled when a violent shaking jerked her back to consciousness, was the salty sweet smell of John Smith's skin. She was sure she had died with her nose up against his bare, tanned thigh just above the knee. Inwardly, she recoiled in embarrassment, even as she noticed the long, wide planks of a great ship at eye level. It slapped dangerously up against the skiff. She looked up. An exhilarating sweep of joy almost sank her back into the bottom of the boat. All at once, Smith was shaking her arm and there were scrambling seamen all about, like squirrels dashing through treetops. Someone put a bottle of something cold and wet to her lips, and she swallowed a precious mouthful of ale before coughing it up. Just the sensation of it dripping down her chin made her want to faint with relief.

"Up you go now," said Smith, his once solemn voice filled with happiness. He lifted her by the waist with what little strength he had left, and their eyes locked when the sea bounced them back together, nose to nose. Before she could tear her gaze away from his dark green stare, smellier arms pulled her up into a chair that bumped and thumped against the starboard side of a massive ship of the line. She was heaved heavenward, saved from the little skiff at last.

Perhaps the ship looked massive because she was at the waterline, but as her liberators towed her up deck by deck, she estimated it to be as big as the ship that had brought her from England. She held tight to the ropes, her arms trembling with fatigue. To fall now would mean certain death because she did not have the strength left to swim.

With a final heave to, the chair crossed over the bulwark, and a flurry of crew members helped her down onto a smooth, clean deck. A billowing Union Jack and long, gay streamers snapped in the wind high up on the mizzen mast. Men everywhere in slops and caps hurriedly obeyed orders from a shouting bosun. She searched the stern for a captain or lieutenant, and there he was. Standing tall at the con with his black cocked hat and polished epaulettes stood the captain of her salvation. Perhaps he knew her uncle personally.

The trio of helpful men who'd helped her to her feet on deck fell back. Julia realized with horror they were surprised to see her in nothing but a damp, stained shift. She was dirty and unkempt and did not look like an admiral's niece. She crossed her arms over herself with embarrassment, and the men dropped their eyes. A heavy blue coat fell across her shoulders. She looked up into the chiseled face of the captain. He smiled, and his eye crinkled at the corners even as they sparkled with some unspoken enthusiasm.

"Are you ill?" He had a gentle voice, smooth and baritone.

Julia shook her head, unable to speak. His kindness felt like a healing balm to her soul. His ship and his rescue were a gift that so filled her with gratitude she could drop to her knees and hug his boots.

"I am Captain Dewey of His Majesty's, *Triumph*. Welcome aboard, Miss...?"

Wavering on her tired legs, Julia whispered, "Miss Julia Scott. Miss Julia Scott of Netley Hall and niece of Admiral Hammond."

The captain's coffee brown eyes widened at her claim, but he did not miss a step in their introductory dance. He bowed deep, and the officers trailing behind him did so as well. Julia smiled. She had not been bowed to with such formality since her last ball. Of course, it had really been nothing more than a country dance. Caroline had permitted her to attend as long as she accepted a dance from every gentleman who asked her, no matter his age or station.

"This way," Captain Dewey said. He swept his arm toward the aft cabin nestled under the poop deck and called to his lieutenant, "Have Mrs. Lovejoy see to this young lady." His attention returned to Julia. "The cooper's wife will make you comfortable."

Julia dropped a curtsey. She let her eyes linger on the young captain as she was led away. He'd watched her, but only for a moment. There were other things to see to, she knew, things like John Smith. With a start, Julia searched the crowd of seaman. Smith stood among them, even as the Captain strode over with the bosun at his heels. He was in good care now, she hoped, but she swallowed back a lump of fear. Doubt crept into her heart. When they realized what he was, what would they do?

THE COOPER'S WIFE, Mrs. Lovejoy, appeared to have as happy a disposition as her name; at least she was pleasant and smiled a great deal of the time. After helping Julia eat a little broth and scrub herself clean, the woman took it upon herself to comb out the snarled knots on Julia's wild and tender head. With a long braid coiled around her crown, only the shocking shade of Julia's nose made her look like a heathen. Mrs. Lovejoy complimented her on her bright blue eyes, and with a cheerful grin offered to share a worn and dark simple dress.

"You were traveling alone?" the woman asked in astonishment. Her gray hair was knotted on the top of her head, and her plump rosy cheeks reminded Julia of Mrs. Williams.

"Not exactly." Julia related her journey with Mrs. Williams and how she fell ill and chose to stay in Nassau. With Caroline's letters and her own papers, Julia had decided to continue her voyage under the care of Captain Hayward as planned, a trusted acquaintance of her father and family.

"Upon my word," the lady said with pity, "you have been tested by the Lord."

"And He's seen fit to preserve me," Julia smiled back. It melted away when she wondered what had become of poor Captain Hayward.

"Well, you've a new guardian angel now, I reckon." She grinned again as if an unspoken secret hid in Julia's heart. She didn't know if the woman referred to herself, the captain, or even Smith.

She turned about so the lady could tie back the simple, illfitting gown. She could not pretend she did not feel... something about her rescuer. She had not explained what Mr. Smith had been doing aboard a ship full of pirates, or where he had come from. Truth be told, Julia did not know herself. He wore the clothes and kept the company, but somehow like with the island natives, he seemed distanced from it all.

He has been kind indeed, she answered at last, diplomatic yet truthful. She nibbled her lip, and it stung. She would be spoiled with food and rest while the unfortunate Mr. Smith would be stowed below deck in chains. She worried herself into a fitful sleep, but slept for a prolonged time. When she could force her eyes to open, Mrs. Lovejoy was there with more water and a matronly hug. She drifted back into dreamless oblivion, wondering at the kindness of the most unexpected people. Was she naive or had her stepmother ruined her completely?

The sun beamed through the one great porthole in Julia's quarters when she stretched and came to at last. She shared her little space with a fat, roly-poly cannon. It had not surprised her, but it felt strange to sleep beside a gun that shot hot, black metal balls at other vessels. If the drums began to beat, she knew she would be turned out immediately, and her little bed would disappear into a bulkhead. She had no things anymore. Her two trunks had been lost with Captain Hayward, but she would not complain. She had been spared for some reason, so she would put on a brave face just as she had when Caroline had told her if she would not marry Mr. Carver, she would be sent away to the far side of the world.

Julia sighed, rolling over in her little bed, thankful for its cushioning compared to wooden beams or the sandy, hard ground. A small living was all that remained for Caroline since Julia's father had passed. Their home, Netley Hall, was beyond even her control as it fell to Hiram to see to its care. If Hiram had been himself, like before Papa had passed, he would have let Julia stay and depend on her inheritance, but his letters decreed he would relent to all of Caroline's counsel. With what he claimed was reluctance, he'd agreed Julia had to go if she refused to marry and make her own future.

A tear leaked from the corner of her eye and trickled down into her ear. How unfair life could be. Try as she might, she could not make her brother understand that she had no opportunities to find a match locked within the manor's old walls. He seemed to care for nothing but squandering away all of his income, and Caroline would not spend a farthing on gowns or bonnets, much less a Season. That left only local bachelors who were lifelong friends or acquaintances, but there was no time for a sheltered girl to find a love match in so short a time. She had done little and gone nowhere and, besides a deep affection for her father's stable boy, had never been smitten enough to give her heart away.

A curt knock at the narrow hatch forced Julia to sit aright. She pulled a thin blanket up in modesty although she was dressed in Mrs. Lovejoy's clothes. "Yes?"

The woman herself peeked in. "The captain would like you to join him to dine." She smiled.

Conscious of her rumpled clothes Julia patted her hair down. "I'll help you freshen up," Mrs. Lovejoy promised. Pleased, Julia nodded. Her chaperone shut the door and left her to stretch her legs and gather her thoughts.

Dinner with the captain. What a privilege, she acknowledged with pleasure. She had dined with Papa's good friends when he was alive, so there was no need to feel intimidated. Better yet, without Caroline's penetrating presence, there would be no one to subject her to insecurity about her looks or her dependence on everyone else. But she was, she discovered, anxious after all, when Mrs. Lovejoy repaired the damage the long nap had done to her hair. Her borrowed gown was too large and not appropriate for dinner, but there were no other options, and she could not be rude.

The officers around Captain Dewey's table stood when a steward ushered her in. She curtsied and tried to keep the blush from her cheeks. The ship swayed, and Julia caught herself on the back of a chair. The steward withdrew it for her to sit, and the company seated itself around the table once more. Before she could draw her breath, the service was passed with a tureen of soup. The steward filled a crystal glass with a suspicious drink.

"Are you rested, Miss Scott?" Captain Dewey inquired. All faces at the table turned their gazes toward her as one.

She nodded. "I thank you, sir." He beamed. His eyes momentarily dropped to her neck and shoulders.

"Allow me to introduce my men." Captain Dewey collected himself, while Julia blushed again at his obvious distraction.

He went around the table, acknowledging his lieutenants, bosun, purser, chaplain, and ship's surgeon, as well as one rather mature midshipman.

"Gentlemen," the captain finished, "our lovely guest and survivor is the niece of the distinguished Admiral Hammond. We are gathered tonight to honor her and celebrate her safe return to civilized company."

The men in the room nodded and raised their glasses. Since none of their jaws dropped in shock, Julia assumed her identity had spread through the ship like fire. They turned to their evening meal, and between her best attempts at small sips of turtle soup, Julia explained as delicately as she was able how she had been taken by pirates and John Smith had come to her aid.

"John Smith?" The captain chuckled and looked around the room. The officers joined him in quiet laughter. They seemed to know the details of her misadventure already. Julia's gut sank like a stone. The soup did not seem as heavenly as it had at first taste.

"He is..." she began, then, "Is he well?"

Captain Dewey's mouth curled in a patronizing but kind smile. "He is well enough, but too ill to join us for dinner."

Julia understood his meaning. Of course he would not be allowed to join them. It did not matter whom he had rescued.

He was a criminal and would hang to pay for his crimes. She shuddered.

"Are you ill?" whispered the lieutenant beside her, and she gave a negative toss of her head. Inhaling, she determined to finish her meal and be as proper as one would expect of an Admiral's niece. She tried to force her concerns about Smith from her mind. It was not easy. She would speak to her uncle as soon as she possibly could do so.

After several courses including sea pie and syllabub, fruit and cheese and wine, she excused herself when she realized the officers waited for her to leave. For a West Indies ship of the line, Julia felt she could not have possibly eaten better.

She smiled and thanked them all, sure to be attentive to Captain Dewey. His square shoulders bowed low and proper when she retired from the room. Had she imagined the sparkle in his eye? He took notice of her during the meal, careful to turn the conversation her way if anyone began to yammer on about something that made no sense to her. There was a feeling of elation in her heart for their kindness, and gratitude to be out of the sun and danger at last. People were still good, and people were kind. Despite Caroline and pirates and even strange flesh eating savages, there was still hope in her world.

Mrs. Lovejoy tiptoed in with a small lantern after Julia took a turn around the deck with a midshipman at her arm. The *Triumph* was a beautiful ship, as fine as its captain, properly maintained, and in order. The gangly boy pointed out the hand-carved figurehead leading the ship westward toward the colonies, the spectacular height of the mainmast crow's nest, and then at last the beautiful waning moon, glimmering in the onset of twilight. He walked her to her quarters and she thanked him, flushing again at the look of adoration he would not disguise. It made her chuckle to herself once alone in her quarters. She was surely a few years his senior, and he could not be eighteen. Apparently there were far more young ladies in England than at sea.

When Mrs. Lovejoy arrived to help her undress, Julia felt she could almost relax as her hair was brushed to a soft, full shine. "We'll reach English Harbor before sunrise, God willing," said Mrs. Lovejoy.

Julia smiled to herself. Wearing nothing but her laundered shift and a pair of long, borrowed stockings, she embraced a surge of happiness.

"Your uncle will be there, I'd wager. They'll send word ahead, you know."

"No, I did not," Julia said. "I'm sure he will be shocked. He expected me to travel with Captain Hayward, but where the ship is now I don't know."

"Oh, they'll find it," Mrs. Lovejoy said. "Those filthy beasts won't keep her for long."

"Well, there was fire, you see. I don't know there is anything left to be found." Julia frowned. "I'm lucky to have survived, to be here at all."

With a quick twist and a knot of Julia's hair, Mrs. Lovejoy turned Julia about, and affectionately pushed loose tendrils of hair behind each of her ears. "You have come a long way to us, Miss Scott. Your uncle will be overjoyed to have you in Antigua."

Ignoring all expectations of her class, Julia put her arms around Mrs. Lovejoy's neck and gave her a squeeze. "I did not know what I would find over the sea and so far from home, but you give me hope, Mrs. Lovejoy, you and—" She almost added Mr. Smith to her list of inspiration but caught herself. She dropped back down onto the end of the cot.

"What it is?"

"It's just..." It felt like iron bands cinched tight around Julia's chest. It almost pained her to breathe.

Mrs. Lovejoy's face crumpled with concern. She put a short, stout finger under Julia's chin. "Yes?"

"Do you know the man who was with me in the skiff? Where have they put him away?"

A wide grin spread across the cooper's wife's face. "Good heavens, Miss Scott. Your poor angel is in the sick-bay."

Relief showered over Julia like spring rain. They did not know. Whoever or whatever they thought Smith was, at least he was being cared for. The heat and the labor of his rowing, and his insistence to sit or stand to shield her from the sun, had left him as close to death as she. How he had endured it she did not know, for she had in one long moment, surrendered and wished for death. The memory of her cowardly behavior made her cheeks hot.

Mrs. Lovejoy patted her on the knee. "Your handsome hero is well enough, I promise you." She grinned slyly even as Julia said, "Oh, no, I—" but the woman laughed. "He was eating a bowl of steaming burgoo when I left him last, and soon as he can keep something down, I'm sure he'll be let out."

Julia did not ask to where he would be left or what would happen next. She pressed her lips together to restrain from any-more reckless inquiries. Whatever the captain and his crew as-sumed about Smith, she would not inform them otherwise. He may have been violent and uncouth, but he had treated her with integrity. Besides, Mrs. Lovejoy herself seemed to approve of him well enough, or at least she didn't harbor any suspicion.

The kind woman retired and with a murmur of "good-night" left Julia to the cool, dark night. Her soul felt calm and peaceful even if she was in a tiny room on a giant ship in the middle of a vast sea. She closed her eyes and thought about morning. Her uncle would be waiting. She would tell him all of Caroline's deeds, Hiram's tomfoolery, explain how John Smith had risked his life to rescue her, and somehow, all would be well at last.

JULIA AWOKE TO THE repetitive gong of the ship's bell and the scurry of bare feet overhead. She loped out of her rough-and-ready bed and washed herself quickly down with a pitcher of water and a clean cloth. Pausing, she stood still as a deer, her feet spread apart to balance herself against any un-expected sways. The sound of water lapping against the outer beams was all her straining ears could hear over the voices of men and seabirds. There was a general hum of excitement aboard, and she realized the ship was not moving forward, but idle, as if anchored down and swinging on a morning tide.

A knock on the door announced her late breakfast. "Have we arrived?" she asked, and a small boy nodded then grinned like he had mischief up his sleeve. She thanked him and gob-bled down her eggs. She waited impatiently for Mrs. Lovejoy, and the two of them scurried up topside to the warm sunshine and stunning turquoise sea views of English Harbor.

"Just there." Mrs. Lovejoy pointed as they stood alongside the ship's bulwark out of harm's way. "That's the battery where the army keeps watch."

Julia studied it with interest. It sat nestled on the highest hill above the port, and ribbons of green trees stretched out around the island in either direction. The port itself bustled with fervent activity. Various ships in every shape and size bobbed like paper boats grown to gigantic proportions. Aboard the *Triumph*, they looked rather small, but Julia knew if she were closer they would swallow her up and block out the sun.

The bosun blew the captain's call and all hands came to attention. Julia turned, smiling with expectation. Captain Dewey strode from his cabin, a midshipman dogging his heals. The boy was not smiling and neither was the captain. He did not go above deck to the con, but made a beeline for Julia with a grim look she could not help but dread.

When he halted, the look in his eye made her shiver with anxiety. They had discovered the truth of John Smith. Someone must have guessed at what he was. Her heart sank to the soles of her scruffy, borrowed boots. She cast a hopeful look over her shoulder, but did not see any officers waiting for her on the quay, much less an admiral.

Captain Dewey bowed stiffly then seemed to catch himself. "Miss Scott," he said. A look of disapproval could not be misinterpreted.

Swallowing in alarm, Julia dropped a low, deep curtsy.

"I expect you will give me your real name now?"

Stunned, Julia tried to understand his meaning. He held a piece of parchment aloft, with a dangling ribbon and broken seal. "I don't understand. Is my uncle not here?" she asked.

The captain's frown deepened. "I know you are not who you claim to be, Miss. If you cannot give me any proof or other information, I will have to..." He glanced down, examining her like he had at dinner. "Despite your fine appearance and manner of speech," he continued, "I've been assured you are not the niece of Admiral Hammond."

Even as she could not believe her ears, Julia noted he seemed to tremble with humiliation or anger. His hands were tight fists.

"I assure you," she responded, with rising alarm, "I am who I say. I may not be dressed properly, but I have lost all that I own." She reached out and clutched Mrs. Lovejoy's arm for support and the woman squeezed back to comfort her.

"Beggin' your pardon Sir, Captain Dewey," Mrs. Lovejoy said in a toneless voice, "perhaps there has been a misunderstanding."

The captain shook his head and looked offended at her suggestion. "I've word from the admiral, and he assures me his only living niece is in Southampton and is not expected in the Indies."

Julia gasped. Her legs nearly buckled beneath her. Of all the cold and cruel calculations, how could Caroline send her off under such pretenses?

"My stepmother, Mrs. Scott of Netley Hall, wrote him last Easter, and I have been invited."

"Do you have papers?"

"Of course I do not," Julia cried. "It is as I told you. I've lost everything."

Behind them a lieutenant put his hand to his mouth and cleared his throat loudly. The captain spun sharply on his heel. "What?" His voice cracked like a lightning bolt. The crew around them winced then commenced to work harder and faster while pretending not to listen. The officer stepped back and the captain joined him for a conference. Grimacing, he nodded and turned back to the ladies.

"Mrs. Lovejoy, you are dismissed. Young woman, you are fortunate that Mr. Greenway has offered to take you ashore."

No words of self-defense would form in her mind. Julia clung desperately to Mrs. Lovejoy, who pitied her with teary eyes and another pat.

"But I am Julia Scott," Julia insisted.

The officer ignored her and returned to his duties. Captain Dewey cast her one last look of distaste before angrily shouting an order that did not make any sense. His words and their meaning were drowned out in the shock of her situation. Julia's ears buzzed. Her face burned with humiliation. Mrs. Lovejoy patted her once more and with a sorrowful look said, "You take care, my dear."

Julie clutched at her arm, horrified at the act of desperation even as her fingers curled around the woman's wrist. "I am Miss Scott, and Admiral Hammond is my uncle." Tears threatened to spill over her eyes, but Julia fought to contain them.

"Come now," said the cooper's wife. She motioned toward the quay. "You won't be all alone." She pressed her lips together and smiled faintly at something over Julia's shoulder.

She looked, hoping against all hope for salvation. To her utter surprise, John Smith stood a few feet away, his dark, cropped hair tamed somewhat with a bit of wax, and his face clean and shaven except around his ears. He wore acceptable attire for polite society, at least a fresh pair of breeches, white linen shirt, and a tailored brown coat. His boots shined as bright as an officer's.

"Good heavens," scolded Julia through her watery eyes. "What are you about now?"

"Miss Scott," he said with a formal bow. "It seems that once again, I am destined to rescue you from distress." He made it sound like a joke.

"But..." Julia couldn't very well shout out the fact that he was a sea rogue. Yet the amusement she detected in his dark, green eyes made her want to shriek out like a lunatic. She was who she said she was. This John Smith, this wild savage, this Mr. Greenway who dressed like a gentleman, was not. And the most maddening thing of all was her heart pattered with happiness as if she should be happy to see him!

CHAPTER FOUR

S he hesitated. Eyes from every direction watched her response. Mrs. Lovejoy gave her a gentle nudge toward the gangway. In two confident strides, Smith marched across the deck to meet her, extended his arm and gave her a sly wink. She half-expected him to pull a wig from his pocket, pat it on his head, and sashay down to a coach and four. Glancing over her shoulder, Julia realized Captain Dewey had disappeared. She sighed, tried to smile for Mrs. Lovejoy, took the arm of the lunatic beside her, and made her way to the dock with her head held high. In her mind she could see Caroline shaking her head in contempt. It was another fine mess.

Smith gave her hand a little pat as they walked down the busy quay arm in arm. "I never doubted you."

She cringed. "Hush up. I am who I say."

Sailors and officers in their path would stop, stare, and then look away when Smith met their appraising glances. "You're making quite an entrance to English Harbor," he remarked. He sounded amused.

In her worn gown and ridiculously large bonnet, Julia was certain she was indeed quite a sight. "I'm fully aware I'm a filthy mess." Once she started she couldn't stop herself. "I have no clothes, no papers, and no money. This is all a grave error."

"I'm sure it is." Smith glanced at her from the corner of his eye. "At least your hair is combed."

"If you would help me find my uncle, I'm sure you will be compensated for your troubles, and who are you supposed to be now anyway?"

"Oh, you did not hear?"

"I did hear, John Smith, and I don't believe you are a Mr. Greenway, not one jot or tittle. Where did you get those clothes?"

"Well, I'm happy to hear you have established a healthy suspicion at last for what you hear and see. I'm properly dressed because I was ashore at dawn and did not sleep in like an old fussock."

"What is that supposed to mean?"

"Good day, Mr. Greenway." A man in dark clothes, wig, spectacles, and top hat, hurried almost past, stumbling over his feet to pause to greet them.

Smith smiled and bowed. "Mr. Tally. How is your wife?"

The thin man answered with "Well, well. Yes, she is well. You are back from another adventure, I see?"

Smith did not reply but bowed again. "Might I introduce you to Miss Julia Scott? I have the honor of escorting her to our esteemed assemblyman."

Julia felt her face fall and stomach roll over.

"Well, well, I say." Mr. Talley looked closer at Julia and her simple attire. Unimpressed he said, "I must be on my way." He held up a packet of mail for Smith to see. "Accounts, of course."

"Yes." Smith looked over his shoulder at the fluttering sails in a row. "Yes, I understand completely."

The two men bowed again and off the elder hurried as if late for an important consultation.

Smith reclaimed Julia's arm, and they walked up a steep flight of boarded stairs that angled back and forth this way and that until they reached a sandy road dotted with carts and carriages. The odor of horse manure wafted along with the breeze, overpowering the familiar smell of tar and fish Julia had grown accustomed to.

"Where are you taking me, *Mr. Greenway*?"

"As I told the last busybody, to meet an assemblyman who may be of some use to you."

Julia stopped walking. "You were serious? We can't just march up to an assemblyman of the Leeward Islands."

Smith laughed and continued, tugging her along. "I most certainly can."

"I have no papers. He won't believe me if he'll see me at all."

"I believe you."

"That's not enough." Smith had completely lost this mind. Whatever nefarious plans he aimed to accomplish while in Antigua must not involve any officials. He'd be discovered and hung for sure. As much as she abhorred the life he chose to live, she did not want him to die. He had good in him. She knew it. A horrible thought flowered in her mind. They might assume she was his companion. His...

Her mind shrank at the idea. Perhaps they would punish her, too. She shook her head vehemently to dispel the horrifying possibilities. "We must not go there. It's too bold. It would be suicide for us both."

"Miss Scott, I assure you, we will be met with open arms." Smith smiled to himself.

Dread splashed over Julia like dirty bath water. She glanced up the ridgeline dotted with dwelling places and swallowed. Her steps became smaller, and her pace slowed. Mr. Smith urged her on under the steaming sun, almost dragging her through the bustling streets crowded with islanders donning far more comfortable and suitable clothing than her own.

"I'm sure it won't do." She tried to think of some better plan that would not inconvenience Smith nor endanger herself. "I'm not fit to be seen in an official's home."

"Well, it's not a government house exactly," Smith explained. "The Caribs burned that down long ago."

"The who?"

"Caribs. The natives. Like our friends we met on the lovely, hilly cay."

"You mean your friends who wanted to eat me."

Smith laughed. It sounded foreign to her ears; so normal and relaxed. "I must confess," he said in a penitent tone, "I was only teasing you. There are no cannibals in the West Indies contrary to popular rumors."

"What?" Julia stopped again, this time in the shade of a tall tree with wide, fingery fronds. "You lied to me?"

Smith tossed his head, still grinning. "I changed it around a bit, you see." He squinted, as the dark leathery hat could not keep out the sun's glare. "The Caribs aren't cannibals at all. Pierre didn't want to have you for dinner, he wanted to have you for life. He asked me for your hand, and I refused. He was unhappy of course, so I thought it best we make our departure."

"In the thick of night and without supplies?"

"It seemed best at the time. I made the incorrect assumption we would cross paths with a ship sooner than we did."

Julia wiped beads of sweat from her upper lip. It trickled down her back and thighs. She'd be soaked through before long. "Well, I suppose that isn't as shocking as wanting to dine *on* me instead of *with* me." Smith grinned at her jest. "Yet, it's frightening all the same." She jabbed him with her elbow rather than give him the smack he deserved. "You should have told me the truth after all. I don't know quite what to make of you, Smith."

He chuckled again. The road became steep and took more effort to scale. "We're almost there," he said cheerfully, ignoring Julia's heavy breathing and the perspiration she rudely swiped away from her temples.

She looked up. They'd passed simple and worn little crate-like homes barely standing to impressive stone edifices with lovely gated gardens. "Why do you think the assemblyman will help us?"

"After all we have been through together, you still doubt me?"

Julia sniffed. "Of course I doubt you."

A crowd of women, darker than the Caribs, moved slowly down the road. They carried colorful baskets on their heads and their bodies were wrapped in light colored linens stained the color of sand.

"Who are they?"

"Slaves," Smith replied.

"Oh." Julia peeked back over her shoulder. She felt a pang of pity and then something else. Shame. "They aren't free at all?"

"No," Smith said curtly.

"It doesn't seem quite right, does it?"

"No, it does not, Miss Smith, and many people think so."

Julia wrinkled her brow. What would Caroline say about slaves in the West Indies? Much like the dangers of French battleships, she hadn't mentioned them at all. Her attitude regarding the lower class at Netley Hall was clear: people were born to their stations in life, and it was their responsibility to live up to them at their best. Yet, it couldn't be true. If it were, Julia would have felt right about marrying a rich old widower even when she could not bear his company.

Caroline had made Julia an example of her ideologies. She was not a boy, would not inherit the Hall, and as such, it was her duty to marry well so that she could be provided for as well as support her stepmother and the Hall should Hiram fail to do so. Mr. Carver had been Caroline's idea, and she'd placed high hopes on the match. The older, balding gentleman spoke loud, laughed loud, and ate loud. He didn't have a title, but he had money, and though it was from trade and not family fortune, Caroline didn't mind one bit.

They stopped at the gate of a beautiful stone manor. It sat heavily on a solid foundation with a long veranda flanked by a dual staircase. The grounds were swept and tidy. Brilliant pink and purple flowers cascaded over trellises and shrubs. It was no English countryside estate, but impressive all the same. In its own way, it fit beautifully into the surroundings. If she had not been penniless and without papers to recommend or prove her identity, she may well have been excited to meet the official.

"After you," Smith said with a refined air. Julia made a face at his sudden manner of gentility. She'd seen him unwashed and half-naked. She'd seen him comatose with fatigue and pale with hunger and thirst. When she made no attempt to cross the yard and take the steps ahead of him, Smith took her arm again, but this time with no formality. Her heart pattered with anxiety. Her stomach cramped with the sharp, cutting pains she'd suffered since Papa's death. It seemed whenever she got her feet beneath her some horrid act of fate pulled them out from under her again.

Two tall and narrow front doors opened before Smith could ring the bell. A solid old fellow with wizened skin stood before them. A smile gleamed as bright as the noonday sun. "Master Greenway," he said with obvious pleasure. "You are back."

Smith looked like he would throw his arms around the man if he could. Instead he said in a familiar voice, "I am back again, Roberts, and I've brought a guest."

The servant bowed slightly at Julia. He still smiled so wide his worn teeth showed, but his eyes were taking her in from head to toe. A look of doubt clouded his eyes. "And will the lady—"

"The lady will need a comfortable room."

The butler retained his expression of suspicion as Julia passed through the front door into a cool corridor. "He's in his study," he said, speaking to Smith. "Shall I announce you?"

"No, do let me surprise him."

Smith spun to his left and pushed open another pair of narrow doors. A fruity breeze tempered with something floral, flooded out into the hall. Befuddled, Julia pressed her lips together in what she hoped was a polite smile as she trailed closely behind Smith.

They crossed a thick Persian rug and stopped in the middle of an oval room. It was white washed and stone with elegant paintings on the walls and fine furniture shipped in from the

Orient. An elderly man looked up from a blue velvet covered chair. It was tucked behind a large oak desk covered with documents, ink bottles, and a slender vase holding a bouquet of white flowers. He raised a hand to his mouth in surprise.

"George Henry Greenway, you worthless devil," he said with undisguised affection. Where have you been since Michaelmas? I'm still receiving your posts and business is out of order."

Smith bowed slightly, a bemused expression on his face. "You would not believe it, Sir, but that is for a later time. Please, allow me to introduce my acquaintance." He waved a hand toward Julia. "Miss Julia Scott of Netley Hall and niece of Admiral Hammond."

Silence. Julia couldn't breathe.

"Miss Scott," Smith continued, turning toward her and making an elegant hand flourish toward the gentleman behind the desk, "My cousin, Sir Henry Gordon."

Cousin? The hot, surging emotion in Julia's middle shot straight up her spine, into her head, and flowered out across her cheeks. She didn't know whether to collapse in relief, scream in outrage, or double over with laughter.

JULIA STRIPPED DOWN to her stained, worn shift and collapsed on a luxurious bed. A sheer curtain of mosquito netting wrapped around the four bed posts made her feel like she'd fainted in a cloud. She stared up at a colorful ceiling painted peacock green. Her mind worked through the chain of events that had carried her away from the stinking, cold naval port of Portsmouth to an elegant bedroom in an assemblyman's home in the tropics. Like her father's death, Hiram's addictions, and Caroline's campaigns, it was madness. The whole world had gone mad, and John Smith, or George Henry Greenway—whoever he was—led the charge.

"THIS IS MADNESS," JULIA cried. She fled the drawing room and sped up the stone stairs to her small wing. She could not shut the bedroom door because of Caroline at her heels. Her stepmother pushed it sharply toward its frame, but caught it before it could slam.

"You ungrateful brat!" she hissed, as if Mr. Carver could hear them all the way from the drawing room. "He made you a fine offer. He has danced with you and courted you for months. Don't you dare make me look like a fool."

Julia found herself backed against the wall, unsure what her stepmother would do. The rage in the woman's flashing eyes was frightening. Julia had rarely seen her lose her temper. When Papa was alive, Caroline controlled herself, sometimes throwing things or rebuking sharply, but with time she seemed to care less and less about who she wounded.

Julia's chin quavered to fight back tears. "I cannot do it. I cannot. He's old and... unappealing." She did not want to say ugly, but Mr. Carver did not appeal to her. He was fleshy and pale, with almost no hair under his tightly curled wig. He smelled like eggs and day old toast.

"He may not be a young, handsome buck, but he's willing to take care of you!" Caroline took a step closer, and Julia could see a pulsing vein throbbing violently in her neck. "He's got money," she whispered, as if it would tempt her, "and you'd have an estate."

"I don't want an estate." Julia curled her hands into fists. She wasn't a rebellious spirit, but stubbornness was her Achilles heel when something frightened her. She did not know how to be any more clear. "I will marry, Caroline. I promise, but I cannot marry him."

"You're past nineteen." Caroline spat. "You will not be young forever and then no one will want you."

Julia's heart sank at the idea. She already knew what it was not to be wanted. She had known since her mother had died, and then Papa, and when Hiram had left her to go on his Tour.

"I will marry," Julia promised, "when I find the right one." If only Caroline would allow her to go to London for a Season or Bath, somewhere, to find others her own age.

"You stupid girl," her stepmother snapped. "The right someone has fortune and connections, like your Papa." She meant to make an example of him and his goodness, but Julia could not help but wonder at Caroline's true intentions settling for a widower with two children. Had Papa's living and Netley Hall been Caroline's only reason for marrying into their happy family?

Indignation erupted in Julia's chest. "You marry him!" Her stepmother took a step back, and her face curled in revulsion. Julia could not contain herself. "You're still young, almost as young as me. You marry Mr. Carver if he's such a catch. I will not."

Caroline's hand slapped her hot flushed face, hard and clumsy. Julia slumped to the floor with her hand over her cheek.

A PROPER YOUNG MAID brought Julia a change of clothes for dinner. Where the undergarments, gown and ribbons came from, she could not guess. The West Indies was one mystery after another.

Julia had taken tea and a long nap, and thus was so rested she felt almost guilty. She smiled at the maid and did not complain as she awkwardly helped her dress. The sweet girl informed her that the lady of the house had been out and would meet her at dinner. She was escorted to a small parlor at the front of the house which she guessed acted as a drawing room for visitors, too. Like Sir Henry's study, it was light and airy. Lonely and feeling quite out of place, Julia situated herself on a cream settee and tried to enjoy the view through the slatted windows until she met the rest of the household.

"I hardly recognized you from behind," said a quiet, kind voice.

Julia turned her head to find Smith, or was it Mr. Greenway, standing at the entry to the drawing room. He leaned his shoulder against the door looking quite relaxed.

She smiled at him, surprised at a feeling of affection that ruffled through her like wind through the trees. "I've had my back to you all this week. Surely, I'm not that different."

"Well, your hair is combed and put up, and you have a rather long neck."

Julia grimaced. "I thank you if you intended that to be a compliment, but before I return my own, you must know I have no idea how to address you."

"'Mr. Greenway' will do." He moved across the room at a slow, thoughtful pace and paused before the windows. "Please proceed with the accolades."

Taken aback she could not think of what to say.

He turned and studied the grounds. "You do like this view better I imagine?"

Julia smiled. "Yes, Mr. Greenway." It sounded foreign on her tongue. "I did not expect to enjoy my time at sea as much as I did, truth be told, however, the last leg of the voyage I found suffocating and hot."

Greenway smirked at something he saw in the yard.

"I like the windows here, too," Julia added. "They pass the breeze but keep out the sun. It's just right."

The gentleman across the room nodded in agreement. He tapped the side of his temple as if thinking.

"Do you live here with your cousin?" Julia was suddenly full of questions.

He turned to face her, hands tucked behind his back as if holding up the window-lined wall. "I do not. I have a home in Falmouth. Modest," he shrugged, "but suitable for a bachelor."

"Oh." It had not occurred to Julia to ask him if he had a wife. She had just assumed he did not.

"You do not sound surprised," Mr. Greenway teased. "You did not think a pirate or savage would be leg shackled?"

"I suppose not." Julia laughed lightly. She could not help it. "My mind was preoccupied with other things, I assure you, like survival."

"You endured it all well."

"I did not. You know I did not."

"I must disagree. You were composed and did not faint or have hysterics."

Julia put a hand to her heart. "I fainted once, and I had hysterics in here."

"I'm sure we both did."

She smiled, although sad for their harsh experience. The loudest question in her mind could not be quieted any longer. "You are not an officer then, I presume?"

Mr. Greenway shook his head. When he did not elaborate she guessed, "A lawyer? A spy?" When he said nothing she teased, "The clergy?"

This made him laugh aloud, and it echoed. Julia winced, wondering at what the servants would think if they heard such unrestrained gaiety.

"Can you envision me in a cassock?" Amusement made Mr. Greenway's eyes light up.

"I cannot," Julia admitted. She could not stop herself from grinning. "I cannot imagine you in many states of proper attire to be truthful."

He laughed, not in the least offended by her cutting words, and moved through the room, taking a seat across from her. "It's all costume, you know. No matter what we wear, it's merely attire to play our parts."

"What is your part?" Julia wanted to know. "What exactly do you do?"

"I own a share of a few of our trade ships here in the Leewards." Mr. Greenway waved a hand. "I assist them at times in some of their affairs."

"I see," Julia said. She had known of such gentlemen before who had traveled with her uncle and dined with her father. "So you are a bit of a merchant—a gentleman after all."

He dipped his chin, and his gaze briefly dropped to the floor. "I thought that was evident when I rescued you from pirates, but yes, I invested my inheritance and turn a comfortable profit." The reference to her former predicament damped her cheery spirits, and it was Julia's turn to study the polished planking on the floor. She scratched an itch on her neck before catching herself. "I didn't mean to upset you," Greenway apologized.

"You did not," she said in the somber quiet. "It's just... I'm glad you did is all. I did not know."

"I know you did not." Greenway drew her eyes back to his with his kind tone.

Julia rubbed her fingers together, smoothing her thumb over a freshly polished nail. "Mr. Greenway, might I ask what you were doing on that pirate ship?"

She thought it might offend him or even make him angry she should wonder at such a thing now, but Greenway put a finger to his chin as if to recollect although she suspected he meant to put her off. "It was a series of unfortunate events," he said at last. "I tend, as you have witnessed, to blend in as best I can when circumstances demand it, you see."

Julia raised a brow with skepticism.

Greenway chuckled again and shook his head. "Miss Scott, you are so quick to believe everything you are told, yet so hesitant to credit me."

"It's not that I don't believe you," she exclaimed.

He put a hand to his chest. "It's all about adaptation," he said trying hard to help her understand. "I was born in the Leewards and have only been to London once in my life. I wear... coats of many colors."

Julia nodded as if satisfied. This was a fact he could not hide, not from her. But as far as any deeper meaning, in truth, she did not much understand who he was now any more than she had at sea.

"MY DEAR LADY GORDON," exclaimed Greenway with pleasure. Before their conversation could delve any deeper into Greenway's situation, a tall woman with tight, fading yellow curls swept into the room. She carried herself with a natural, inviting confidence that made Julia wish for her approval before they were even introduced. She felt grateful Mr. Greenway was there; he took care of the formalities, and when they were both settled comfortably into their seats, the charming lady burst out her apologies.

"You must know I was out for the day," she told them. "Someone is always ill or fretting, and when I have a moment to breathe, the children need me."

"How old is Emma now?" Greenway asked politely.

"My now, let's see." Lady Gordon smiled, and Julia wondered if she was playing or really did not know the ages of her own children. "She is too old for a governess, but not too young to be married."

"I haven't met your children," Julia informed her.

"Oh, my dear," Lady Gordon answered, "they are almost all grown up and married. They keep me young although they are never at home." She patted her cheeks, and Greenway and Julia both chuckled.

"You are from Southampton?" Lady Gordon turned her attentions to Julia, as she had already riddled Greenway with questions about his health and whereabouts.

Julia nodded. "I am. My stepmother thought it would be beneficial to visit with my uncle for a time."

Lady Gordon raised her brows. "The admiral is a busy man. A naval career you know..."

Julia flushed. "I would never impose on him, but I was told I was invited, and I do miss him so." She glanced at Mr. Greenway wondering how much the Gordons knew about her arrival that had not been expected.

As if knowing her mind, he said, "Miss Scott is a favorite of her uncle, but he did not receive the letters from her family who made the arrangements. I've already sent word she is here, and I've assured him we will all watch over her until he returns."

Lady Gordon clapped her hands together. "I am happy to hear it! You must not worry about your good friend." She grinned at Mr. Greenway when she said this, and Julia felt her face redden again. "I'll see that she is properly introduced and chaperoned so much so she will never want to leave us."

Mr. Greenway bowed, and it was apparent he had expected as much from his cousin's wife and without first asking her permission. Blushing with gratitude, Julia opened her mouth to profusely thank her, but dinner was announced, and the trio went out in search of Sir Henry and his table.

It was pleasant, not just because of the many courses or array of exotic fruits and smoked meats, but because of Sir Henry's notice of her and excellent conversation. They discussed Julia's voyage to the Leeward Islands and touched just delicately upon the reason why. She only had to mention curtly that her stepmother had become overwhelmed with her own priorities and had informed Julia her uncle had invited her to stay.

Mr. Greenway said little during her discourse and the apparent interview, but Julia could tell he listened intently. He was probably saving his own questions for later. There was an expression of pity on his face she did not like, when she admitted her father was departed and her only brother preoccupied with personal affairs in town. Both of the gentlemen seemed to get her meaning, and moved on to other more pleasant topics about town and the last Season they had been in London, which Lady Gordon liked very much.

Their anecdotes were entertaining, much like others Julia had heard or read, but they did not salve the shame she carried in her heart that she had never seen London or had a Season. Besides family acquaintances at church and those few in the village she visited on occasion with her stepmother, Julia realized she had never made close friends. By the time the ladies left the men to enjoy their cigars and liquor, she felt small and naive again, like she had for so many years.

She hadn't noticed, she admitted, on her long voyage across the world, she had in her own way become adventurous, determined, and brave when the sea whisked her away from what had been her home. But that all seemed to be fading as she found herself standing again outside some invisible line of society, even if that society was on a primitive isle of the sea. The warm and friendly Lady Gordon made it easier to bear, but it did not diminish the fact Julia was once more a burden for someone else to carry.

She undressed with little help, and crawled into the lovely bed, appreciating the comfort and security of her situation. Who knew how long her stay in the Gordon's home would last. Her mind began to imagine all of the terrible possibilities the next day or week or month could bring. To calm herself and keep apprehension at bay, she remembered Mr. Greenway's commendation that she was composed and not silly. Yes, that was true. She was composed. She did not giggle and act stupidly. Granted, she did not own to all the expectations of a true lady, but there was nothing wrong with composure and solemnity.

Her nerves began to relax, and she snuggled down under the light blanket, grateful for the windows that allowed the night's cool breezes to circulate around the room. It seeped through the mosquito netting that would protect her from vicious insect bites, a pleasure she had not yet experienced. It was curious to be grateful for something so foreign and exotic that she did not yet understand. Much like Smith, she realized. No, Mr. Greenway, she corrected herself. Would she ever get used to thinking of him as a real person?

Clean, shaven, and properly attired in dinner clothes with a loose cravat at his neck, he was captivating and far more fetching than any gentleman Julia had ever intimately known before. It was a clever, rugged handsomeness, not quite like the pretty Captain Dewey, but appealing all the same. She had not met many men outside of Netley Hall, she reminded herself, and was probably too easily impressed by anyone who showed her any kindness. That was Caroline's selfish doing. It had not been that many months, but Julia could see it now.

CHAPTER FIVE

S he slept through breakfast and until the morning chill faded. Her bedcovers felt hot. Julia sat up groggily, wiping
away lose tendrils of hair and eyeing the cheerful, warm room
through the fog of netting settled over her bed. A tray on the
table beside her was covered with a linen cloth. She fumbled
with the netting until she found an opening and lifted the cloth
to find bread, cheese, and more fruit. Her stomach rumbled as
if she hadn't eaten several courses the evening before, and she
chuckled to herself. She hadn't eaten so well since leaving England, and this fare was more exciting and fun. Her hesitant
maid tiptoed in just as Julia was trying to dress herself. The girl
opened a wardrobe and showed Julia three more gowns besides
the borrowed one she'd worn to supper.

Julia covered her gaping mouth with her hand. "Are you
sure? I can wear these?"

The girl nodded, just as pleased to present them to her as
Julia was anxious to wear them. "To whom do I owe my gratitude?" she asked as a sky blue gown with a matching embroidered hem was pulled down over her head.

"Lady Gordon had some put away that belonged to her
daughter, and Mr. Greenway was eager to contribute as well."

"Mr. Greenway?"

"He has connections," her helper explained.

"Indeed he does," Julia said slowly, "all over the West Indies."

The servant's face lit up, and she giggled in agreement. Apparently Mr. Greenway was well liked by everyone in this house, and no one would bat an eye that he would see to her comforts even though they had no family connection. That spoke much about his reputation, did it not? Julia could not picture him behind a desk studying trade routes when she knew about so many of his other... abilities. The memory of the flash of gunpowder and shock the first time she'd laid eyes on the enigma made her frown. Not all of her observations were redeeming. He truly was a man of many colors, and if a red flag meant no quarter then he certainly flew that one well.

She spent the late morning in the drawing room, picking up books and putting them down, gazing out the window, and counting flowers in the fabric of a comfortable chair beside a writing table. Lady Gordon had appointments that could not be changed, and although she invited Julia to join her, it felt too soon to follow her hostess around in her regular routine like a dependent companion.

By noon day, even though the sun was at its peak and the house warm, she could not keep from stepping outside. It was not in her nature to stay indoors and be idle, one of her many shortcomings Caroline tried without success to break. Julia went to her room, grabbed Mrs. Williams' old bonnet, and slipped outside without being questioned or chided. The grounds were grassy and the long drive sandy and peppered with gravel. There were hedges of beautiful tropical flowers in a rainbow of colors with blood red hibiscus planted along the fence line. After exploring around the house, she found a path behind it past the vegetable gardens that led through thin, rabbles of trees until it stopped abruptly, broken off by a sharp incline that dropped precariously down to a narrow strip of river. Following it with the eye, one could see it led almost straight away to the sea with a rocky shoreline too hazardous to explore or enjoy.

"You should know by now not to wander off alone."

Julia jerked with fright, backing away from the ledge and its view. Knowing his voice but still alarmed at the sudden intrusion, she turned on Mr. Greenway with vehemence. "You almost scared me to death. I might have fallen!"

Greenway brushed past her and looked over the edge of a drop that would mean certain injury if not death. "I wouldn't be able to save you from that," he said with raised brows.

"Don't tease me. My heart's still racing."

"I am not teasing you. I've come with a reason." He held up a letter folded neatly over but unsealed. "I have word."

Julia scrunched her brows. "Is it from my uncle?"

"Yes, aboard the *Dunkirk*. His ship you, know."

Julia wondered if he was testing her. "Yes, I knew, I just… He's written again?" She tried to keep the sound of hope out of her tone.

"I wrote him, as soon as we arrived in fact. Captain Dewey sent word ahead, but I was delayed until we reached the island to contact him myself."

"You sent word about me?"

"Of course. I have been introduced to your uncle, although we are not intimate friends. I explained your situation as much as I was able, and although I did not know the details as I do now, I assured him I was convinced you were indeed his niece and that your family had sent you with an understanding you would be under his protection."

Julia laced her hands together and squeezed her fingers. "You've received word from him already?"

"I have." Greenway's lips were set in a straight, grim line.

When she could bear it no longer she exclaimed, "Well, what does he say? Am I still not to be believed?"

"Not at all. He is just northwest of us lying low under the Windwards, which is why we have received word so quickly. He has business to attend to as one would expect, but he thanked me for my communication and promised to see the matter resolved as soon as he is able to return."

Julia waited for relief to pour over her, but it did not come. This improvement gave her hope, but it was not a definite resolution. "Then he believes it, that I am—"

"Whom you claim to be?" Greenway smiled, but it did not reach his eyes. "Surely you know your own name. You will stay under the Gordons' protection until your uncle sends for you. I'm sure there will be more questions as the situation comes to light."

Julia nodded. "Of course."

Greenway stared, like he watched her for a reaction that did not come.

"Thank you," she stammered, aware she had forgotten her manners. "Thank you for everything you have done, Mr. Greenway." She looked down at her pretty gown. "And for this."

He bowed slightly although it seemed silly and impersonal. "It was not a gift should anyone think it inappropriate. I'll settle with your uncle later. As for now, you should not be down here past the grounds." Greenway looked back over his shoulder. "Come along, and we'll have something good to eat on the veranda."

Julia smiled. "You do like something good to eat."

"I often go too long without it."

She nodded, this time understanding his references completely.

SHE TOOK TEA IN THE drawing room with Mr. Greenway, and Sir Henry joined them briefly. It was obvious he was a busy man. Visitors came and went all the day long. Some peeked into the room and examined Julia with curiosity. Others she heard coming and going, including a short, squat secretary with a wig too short to cover his thin, straggling hairs beneath it.

Despite the pleasant conversation at tea and dinner, Julia felt at odds with her situation. The next morning she hoped to see more of the island, but Mr. Greenway had disappeared and like the day before, the assemblyman kept continuous company and his wife had obligations. Julia did not wait for the sun to make the outdoors too hot, she went out soon after breakfast with a loaned parasol, paper, and pencils for sketching. Although tempted to walk back down the incline toward the sandy knoll above the river, she chose instead the shade of a silk cotton tree, so large and twisting and wide she could not put her arms around it. An elegant little chair, while not completely comfortable was already there, as if it were a favorite place for someone in the house to spend their time.

Julia plopped down and surveyed her surroundings. The world seemed fresh and soft, a landscape covered in green and surrounded by azure blue in all directions. Although bright red and orange flowers of every exotic form and flavor punctuated the view, it was the cozy feeling of rest and moderation she relished. There did not seem to be much hurry in this miniature world. There were no rigid expectations and no Carolines with sharp words and exasperated mannerisms. In fact, like her voyage across the ocean, no one seemed to be exasperated with Julia ever at all.

"Except Mr. Greenway," she reminded herself aloud. He'd seemed exasperated with her from the start, although he showed no ill will toward her interruptions of whatever he had been doing in the company of ne'er-do-wells when he rescued her.

"Well," said a smooth, agreeable voice, "you have made yourself comfortable, Miss Scott."

Julia looked up from her drawing of a bougainvillea blossom. Her eyes widened in surprise. "Captain Dewey," she said with bewilderment. "What... How... do you do?" Her cheeks heated with chagrin, and she lowered her head to hide them with her bonnet.

The captain bowed. He was dashingly dressed in uniform, despite his ship resting far below them in the harbor. "I'm well, and I hoped to find you as much. I've business with Sir Henry," he explained.

Julia composed herself and tilted her head to meet his gaze so he did not think her rude or reticent. "I'm well myself, Captain." She tried to smile, but it felt forced. "Mr. Greenway has seen to my every comfort."

"Oh, has he now?" Captain Dewey straightened and grinned. He slipped off his issued black hat, remembering he'd forgotten it, and turned it over and over in his hands. His brown clipped hair was the light shade of tanned deer hide. His dark eyes studied her all the while. "You look quite recovered," he said, "and I am happy to see it."

"Those are kind words for a stowaway aboard your ship."

The captain chuckled. His smile widened, and his cheekbones flushed with good humor. "We must forget all of that, Miss Scott. I was misinformed, and it consumed me with guilt to send you away. A most distasteful task."

"I understand completely. It was an unfortunate mistake."

"A lost post," said the captain, "and a regrettable error. Yet here you are, and as fine and lovely as a cloud."

Julia glanced down at the blue posies scattered across her morning gown. The hem of a new, white petticoat peeked out at her ankle. "I suppose I am a bit blue this morning," she admitted. She tugged on the faded azure ribbons streaming from Mrs. Williams' old bonnet.

"Yes, well," the captain grinned, "I meant your lovely turquoise eyes. They are dark as sapphires under the shade of this tree, and with your bonnet, too."

Julia glanced up at the cool canopy of thick leaves above her head. "Then I must thank the tree," she said, surprised at how easily the retort came to her.

Dewey bowed again. "I must leave you now, but after my appointment at the house, perhaps you would allow me to escort you up the ridge. It's a lovely walk, a bit steep, but I no doubt you're capable enough."

"I find I'm capable of a great many things." Julia nodded her acceptance and watched him stride toward the house and leap up the stairs. He was polite and well mannered, she thought, and especially dashing for a sea captain, not old and shriveled from sun and war. Not yet anyway, she told herself. His attention and regret of her removal from his ship was kind indeed.

Satisfied, she returned to her drawing, and before she could begin another he joined her under the tree again, offered his arm, and together they passed through the gate and climbed the hill arm in arm toward the crest of the spiny Antiguan ridge, where clouds billowed low, tumbling over one another on a wild wind that seemed to swirl and dip into all of the trees and over the distant surf, too.

"How beautiful it is," Julia breathed.

Captain Dewey stood beside her, tilting his head just so that the brim of his hat shaded his eyes. He took in all of the shipyard below and the eternal stretch of sea that reached to the distant horizon.

"It is," he agreed, "and there are more, you know. Breathtaking isles and cays scattered all around the equator.

Julia put her hands on her head to keep her loose bonnet from blowing away. She smiled to herself then at Captain Dewey who'd turned to catch her eye. "I can't decide if it's the view or the never ending breeze that makes it seem like heaven. This must be near to what it's like." Everything felt luscious and clean, warm and sunny.

"Some people find it stifling to be surrounded by water at every turn."

"You do not, I am sure," Julia teased.

"I would not belong on a ship. That is certain." The pair of them laughed. Julia put a hand on her stomach and inhaled. "How can one be stifled by the ocean?" The captain murmured in agreement. She could hardly believe only days before she'd felt abandon and despair when the blue-green waters were all she could see. With land under her feet, and good food and polite company, all of that had changed.

Captain Dewey had nothing but kind things to say about Southampton, where he had often passed through to visit a relative she did not know. He shared with her his childhood dream of naval service from his home in Crawley. Like her, he preferred to be outdoors, and he much enjoyed music as long as he wasn't called upon to play or sing. He missed his horses, and the hunt, he confided, but nothing could compare to the adventure of new lands over the horizon.

"We're kindred spirits," Julia decided. "Every daydream I ever knew was just over the trees, beyond the stream, over the horizon and just out of sight."

"And now you are here," said Dewey. "Perhaps it is fate."

Julia put a hand to her heart. "I have no doubt. My papa loved the sea and took me there often with my brother when I was just a girl. He loved the continent, too, and although he had never been away but once, we read about places all over the world together, and read Uncle's letters, too." Julia smiled at the recollection. "They were fond of one another."

"Do you mean the admiral?" Dewey queried. He'd offered his arm to escort Julia back to the Gordon's home, down the winding road and past towering mimosa trees and views of the harbor.

"Yes, my Uncle Richard. We call him the Admiral you know, to be proper, but he'll always be Uncle Richard to me."

"Are you on good terms?"

"As far as I know."

"It must be some time since you have seen him."

"Yes," Julia nodded. "Not since I was twelve. I think he has forgotten all about home."

"It happens, but you know," said Dewey, patting her arm, "home is where your heart beats at its happiest. It's not always where you were born."

Julia nodded. "I understand. If every day was as beautiful as today, I don't think I'd ever want to leave this place."

This seemed to please Captain Dewey. She caught him sneak a glance at her and quickly looked away. "Those are wonderful words to hear, Miss Scott," he admitted. "Especially to a man who has left home far behind, too."

Julia couldn't help but peek at him and smile at his wistful words. He stared back until she broke the connection. Heat creeped up her cheeks again, but this time from the nervous realization he was being overly kind, and perhaps, overly attentive. It was like with Mr. Carver she realized, like his compliments and examining stares, but this was far better, for Dewey was much younger, and she acknowledged with a tingle in her stomach, far more handsome.

They passed through the gates to the house, and Julia wished she could ask him to tea. It was too early she reasoned, and it was not her place to do any inviting for the Gordon's anyway. Besides, up where the stone steps met the long, wide veranda, stood Mr. Greenway. Julia was not surprised to see him again. She assumed his personal business had taken him away for the day.

He stood at attention, stiff and to his full stature, a hat in his hands and an unnatural frown on his face. Dewey fell silent once they reached the grounds, and Julia wondered at the consternation she felt swell up in her chest.

"Mr. Greenway," the captain said as he handed Julia up the stairs.

Greenway did not bow or return the officer's cheery greeting. "Good afternoon, Captain," was his stone-faced reply.

"I've had the pleasure of the Admiral's niece," said Dewey. He offered a funny, twisting smile and added, "We took a turn about the island. A little bit of it anyway." He turned to Julia. "Next time I'll borrow a carriage."

The idea of seeing the whole island filled Julia with enthusiasm. "That would be marvelous," she admitted. "It's been lovely to explore so far."

"So far?" Greenway said with an odd curl of his lip. "You've just come up the hill from the quay," he said, "and you haven't been here a fortnight."

"Yes, I know." She pursed her lips, annoyed to have him dampen her joy.

He looked her up and down as if he did not know what to think of her new and elegant attire then at the captain as if he'd done something wrong.

"I must take my leave," Captain Dewey said at once. He bowed at Julia and promised, "With your permission, I'll call on you before I sail again."

Taken aback at his use of "permission" and "call" she nodded mutely. He smiled at her again with admiring softness then turned on his heel. She watched him go, not knowing what she should do, but only that she felt elated and anxious and confused all at the same time.

She turned to Greenway to somehow convey her thoughts, but her questioning look dissolved in surprise. He was staring at her with thunder in his eyes and a jaw set in an angry, hard line.

TEA WAS NOT PLEASANT. Sir Henry did not attend, and Lady Gordon did only briefly. She apologized that she had a headache and went to lie down after making certain Julia had a pleasant day. Mr. Greenway stayed longer than Julia expected. His mood did not change from their meeting on the veranda until much after Lady Gordon took her leave.

"One would think you'd had enough equatorial sunshine," he said at last from a narrow backed chair. It was scooted up to a walnut writing desk where Greenway scratched out replies to posts that had arrived addressed in his name.

Julia stepped back from the window where she'd been peeking between the wide slats. "I'm not in the sun," she retorted, "not directly." She glanced at the settee and dull book she had borrowed from the library. "I'm not used to wasting away pleasant afternoons with my nose in a novel."

Greenway laid a pen down and leaned back. "It wouldn't hurt you to dedicate your time to studies of the Leewards." He motioned toward the windows. "The flora and fauna especially, if they interest you so."

"I saw a lizard on the veranda this morning. It was as long as my hand and striped. What do you call it?"

Greenway shrugged.

"Then we both have been derelict in our education."

He frowned, and it troubled her. Julia moved back to the settee, and sat on her side, turning to rest her arms on the back of it so she could face him. "I don't know why you're angry with me, but I won't be here much longer to put you out."

Greenway's face softened. "I'm not angry with you, Miss Scott. I simply don't want to return you to your relative in poor condition. The assemblyman and his wife have taken great pains to help you recover."

"I have," Julia declared. "Except for my complexion, but that will heal in time. I know it looks dreadful." She couldn't help but glance down at her dry, red forearms. Without a shawl, it was impossible to hide the white, peeling skin. She spun back around on the firm cushion beneath her and stared back out across the grounds.

"It does not look dreadful," Greenway muttered from behind her.

A footman entered with a silver tray. Greenway motioned him over, handed him a stack of missives and issued specific instructions. When the post was taken out, he stood and stretched, not knowing that Julia was aware of his every motion. She tried to concentrate on the book she had opened in front of her, but it did not interest her. He came around the settee and settled himself across from her in a different chair. Crossing one leg over the other, he folded his arms.

"What have I done now? You look ready to interview or to scold me."

"Why would I scold you? You are not a child."

"You've scolded me all this day, from the moment I saw you on the veranda."

"I was looking for you," he admitted. "I went down to the knoll over the river. I thought you'd tumbled down the hill."

"Why would I do a stupid thing like that?" Julia smiled to soothe the remnants of his irritation. "I would think by now you know I am as careful as I can possibly be."

Greenway made a face. "I'm aware you aren't obstinate, but that doesn't mean you don't find your way into trouble at every turn."

Julia laughed. "I do not. I've had a stroke of rotten luck." She grimaced. "My mother probably wished it on me."

"I can't imagine a parent wishing their child such ill."

"I meant my stepmother," Julia explained.

"Oh, yes. She is who sent you on your way to the admiral, and without notice."

Julia nodded. "She told me she had written and received word. Perhaps the post was lost or..."

"About your stepmother, she is so overcome as you said with her duties she can't use your help at all?"

Julia raised her shoulders and shook her head at the same time. Exhaling loudly, she closed the book in her lap and ran her finger around the binding. "To be perfectly, honest, Mr. Greenway, I was given a choice, and I chose a new life."

"What was wrong with the old one?"

She looked up surprised to find Greenway serious, his deep set eyes watching her with a mysterious curiosity. "There was nothing wrong with my life, I was perfectly loved. My father died, almost three years ago, and I'm afraid I've become a... a burden to my family."

"You have a brother?"

"Yes, as I told you."

"He inherited but could not help manage your affairs?"

"He lets Caroline manage them for both of us. What's left," Julia added bitterly. She couldn't stop herself. For some reason, she wanted Greenway to know, to understand her circumstances and not to judge her. Rubbing the soft leather of the tome in her lap, she cleared her throat and glanced up at the ceiling beams to collect herself. She would not cry.

"My brother has spent all of his income and accrued some debt. My own inheritance, a dowry, was set aside after Papa's death, but I don't know what's become of it. Caroline does not need the extra expense of my presence, and so she decided I should visit relatives."

"She tossed you out?" The sharp, biting phantom of John Smith reared its head. Greenway scooted down in the chair to rest his head. He raised his brows into teasing dark arches.

Julia bit her lip, considering whether or not to throw the book at him. "Not that it's your business," she said loftily, "but I had a proposal. I chose to come and stay with my uncle instead."

"I see," said Greenway with a wicked grin. "You're one of those chits too stubborn to marry, so your family has sent you away as punishment."

"I am not being punished," Julia shot back, stung at his words, but she recognized it was a lie as soon as she said it. "What I meant was, I had the choice to marry a Mr. Carver or come to Antigua. I had no idea I had not been truly invited." Remorse clouded her features and humiliation warmed her cheeks.

"So Mr. Carver," Greenway asked, picking at a loose thread on the seam of his breeches, "where did he fall short?"

"He wasn't short at all," said Julia. "I simply could not marry a man three times my age even if he had a great deal of money."

Greenway made a face. "That old?" He harrumphed. "That will never do. You're too clever and brave to chain yourself to a walking corpse. Did he like to wander or to sing?"

Julia laughed. "No, neither."

"You have a fine voice," Greenway said decidedly. He straightened in the chair and looked around the room with a sigh. "I hoped to hear you sing again, but I'm afraid I have more reasons for calling on Sir Henry than to receive messages."

"What is it?" Julia's stomach did an anxious roll. "Do not tell me you bring any bad news or there's more scolding for me. I've just found my balance."

"I know." Greenway tilted his head and studied her. "It's not bad news, and it's not scolding."

"I didn't mean it," Julia admitted with a smile. "Today is the first day you've scolded me at all. I suppose I meant teasing."

"Teasing?" Greenway laughed, putting his chin to his hand. "I am a tease, Miss Scott, in every way."

Rather than dissect his meaning, Julia laughed with him. "What is it then?" she said, relieved he had not brought more bad news.

"It's nothing" he said, his face dropping and tone serious. "Only that I have finished my business here and am returning home."

"Oh. Where is that again?"

"Falmouth," he said. "It is just west of here and not too far away should pirates or savages come to call." He smiled at her, and she felt certain she saw fondness in his eyes.

"Well, I'll be sure to send word if they do." They fell silent, Julia unsure of what more say. She was even more hesitant of what his departure meant.

"I've asked Sir Henry to keep me informed," Mr. Greenway told her. The quiet between them did not seem to bother him. They had shared enough of it at sea.

He stood up from his chair in a rather stiff way and reached out to her as if to take her hand. Julia had to lean across the little table at her knees to touch him, but she did so even though it felt formal and silly. Rather than take her hand or give it a squeeze, Greenway brushed his lips across her knuckles and winked.

LADY GORDON JOINED her for dinner, although Julia could do little more than pick at her food. Sir Henry was out, and so they ate alone. When she asked her if she was well, Julia assured her it was just nerves and a little anxiety to receive word from her uncle. She did not wait until dark to retire but excused herself as the sun set low behind the lacy, thin trees and turned the overhead clouds orange and crimson.

Swaddling her bed with the helpful mosquito netting, she fell back on soft, downy pillows and stared into the waning light left in her room. This, too, would be temporary, just as her troubles in the skiff at sea. The uncertainty of not knowing what would happen next left her uneasy. She wondered if it was the word from her uncle or Mr. Greenway's departure that made her feel at odds.

Captain Dewey had promised to call again, but she might well be on her way to her uncle's home on the other side of the island. Why he would not reside right at the harbor was an inconvenient mystery, but after some thought Julia admitted she would not relish the noise or some of the particular company she had observed loitering about the quay. What with all of the taverns and inns and offices and even the battery, one wouldn't have a moment's peace even at sunset.

She sighed and closed her eyes. If her uncle did not find her company convenient, she would have no remaining options. The only solution she could determine, would be to return to Netley Hall and accept Mr. Carver if he would still have her. The thought of it made her ill. She remembered the interest of Greenway's savage host on the small, gravel strewn cay. Perhaps the chief, Pierre, would marry her, she thought with an inward wry laugh.

It was unfair to be forced to make a decision when she not yet one and twenty. She had some years remaining before she would be too far into spinsterhood to be of use. Julia laid an arm across her face, shutting her eyes against a blossoming headache. All she wanted was a roof over her head and to be treated with kindness. She knew love would come, someday. If her father and even Mr. Carver thought her good and smart and handsome enough, then someone else would, too. She just needed to have the right opportunity and God would bring her to someone with whom she could make a life.

Captain Dewey's handsome face and shining epaulettes crept into her thoughts. She didn't want to rush to conjectures any more than she would rush into a situation that would bind her for good, but he was handsome and proper and above all flattering whenever he had her on his arm.

EARLY IN THE MORNING, rattling dishes and a slamming door jerked Julia awake. She lay quietly a few minutes before crawling out of the lavish bed. Sunlight slanted toward the net-covered window in her room, and she saw with pleasure the sky looked peacock blue without a cloud to be seen. Inspired, she chose the light azure gown Mr. Greenway had attained for her, and worried about how and when she would pay him back if her uncle could not. Greenway had not asked for any money, nor had he expected her sincere gratitude. She'd thanked him profusely, but he merely shrugged it off like he didn't mind being forced into the role of benefactor.

She smoothed it down and pulled her hair up, studying her pink cheeks in the long looking glass. Lady Gordon strode in after a brisk knock on her door.

"I was just coming to breakfast," Julia said sheepishly. Her maid left her hair undone and stepped away.

Lady Gordon waved her off. "It's no worry. I had something to tell you and could not wait." She smiled faintly.

Julia braced herself for something tragic.

"I'm afraid we've received following word from the Admiral, and he will not be back for a few more weeks. He's offered to send a cart to move your things and will find you a companion."

"Oh, I see." Julia relaxed on her stool. "I'm afraid I've put him out terribly," she said with a sigh.

"Well, you haven't put me out," Lady Gordon exclaimed. "I've enjoyed your company. Please say you will stay with us a little longer. I can't have you wandering around the far side of the island without officers or our Mr. Greenway to escort you."

Julia chewed her lip, hopeful yet hesitant. "Are you sure it's not inconvenient?"

"Pish! We enjoy having a young lady here with my children grown up and away, and I enjoy the conversation when I'm not out. I haven't left you too bored I hope."

Julia shook her head. "No. You have not." She smiled at her generous benefactress. "I suppose a few more walks and hard study of your husband's library will do me good."

"I'm sure it will." Lady Gordon came around the bed and poised herself in front of the vanity. "I have other news as well. I'm giving a dinner party, and I've invited Captain Dewey late to join us if he's able." She shrugged, her shoulders bared in her silk wrap. "I can't promise he'll accept. Those captains and officers, you know, not a moment to lose and always in a hurry."

Julia nodded, despite thinking Captain Dewey hadn't appeared to be much in a hurry to leave the harbor. His company at dinner would be welcome indeed. There was something about him that made her feel grown up.

"You'll stay then?" Lady Gordon's face lit up with an eager smile.

"Of course, I will," Julia said. She couldn't help but grin back. She hardly could remember ever being treated with such kindness.

TWO FULL DAYS OF WALKING the grounds, studying one of the library's books on ornithology, and writing two copies of a letter to Hiram took up more than enough of Julia's time until the dinner party. She did not tell her brother about Caroline's oversight or of her near capture by pirates at sea. Instead she rambled on about the beauty of the gleaming blue-green water and the smooth, emerald hills rolling over the dusty ivory sand. In her heart she hoped to hear news from home, but she chose to expect nothing from them.

For dinner, she changed into her best dress of blue silk. Lady Gordon's maid braided Julia's hair and coiled it prettily around her crown. She curled the short locks around her temples and offered Julia a small tin of lip rouge to moisten and color her lips.

To Julia's surprise, she felt nervous when announced in the drawing room. It was full of finely dressed gentlemen, most of them older and wigged and chatting amongst themselves like busy monkeys. The conversation halted when she stepped in. It felt as if eyes all around the room burned holes through her.

There were two ladies, both far more fashionable than Julia. They eyed her with something akin to suspicion before turning back to Lady Gordon. Julia curtsied meekly and made a beeline for an empty space on the cream settee. Before she'd smoothed down her frock and completely settled, Lady Gordon introduced her to her two friends, and Julia promptly forgot their names. Captain Dewey appeared at her side. He tipped at the waist, studying her as closely as Lady Gordon's female companions.

"You are a beautiful sight, Miss Scott."

Julia blushed at his compliment, not caring whether it was sincere or contrived. "You've seen this gown before, Captain Dewey," she teased.

"You wear it even better tonight. You are looking much better and fully recovered."

"I am, thanks to the generosity of Sir Henry."

Captain Dewey's eyes twinkled. "I must be off by morning, but I could not refuse an invitation to dine with such a lovely hostess. He glanced at Lady Gordon, and she shook her head disbelieving. "Or her lovely guest," he added.

Julia was tongue-tied. One of Lady Gordon's friends remarked, "You are full of compliments this evening, Captain Dewey."

He straightened and pulled down the hem of his blue coat. "It's the evening air, I'm sure of it," he said with a smile.

"I've never seen you so cheerful," the woman insisted, appraising Julia from head to foot once more.

"He's happy to be ashore," Lady Gordon answered for him.

Julia sank into the settee with relief. Lady Gordon's guests were both married, but they were younger than the assemblyman's wife, and young enough, Julia supposed, to be jealous of anyone who stole away their compliments.

Dinner was announced, and the party filed into the airy dining room in proper order. Julia wasn't surprised to find herself seated next to Captain Dewey, not after Lady Gordon's apparent notice of his continued concern and attentiveness to her guest.

The captain contributed his share of conversation to the party, and even saved Julia from an awkward explanation when one of the gentlemen asked her how she had come to be rescued by Dewey and his men. There was no talk of pirates or savages.

Julia looked around the table at the strangers, and knew they were far more happy to be dining with an official than with her. She realized the night felt incomplete because Mr. Greenway was not there. He had returned to his business and left her in good hands. But, Julia thought with an inward sigh, life was less interesting without Greenway about. In the drawing room, she sat patiently through coffee while the men went off to gamble or smoke or whatever they did when out of sight of the opposite sex.

When she was clearly not a part of the island gossip in Lady Gordon's circle, she meandered out onto the long veranda and found at the far end, a good view of the moon. It lit up the sky like a lantern, reflecting off the harbor below changing ordinary vessels into ghost ships. The evening scent of night-blooming jasmine mingled with the clean, sea air. Julia leaned against a post and stared into the night.

A soft touch on her elbow made her jump. "I'm sorry," said the captain's voice, soft and low. "I didn't mean to disturb you."

"You've discovered me avoiding polite company."

"I think a scene like this is a persuasive excuse."

Julia chuckled. "I was just thinking of home."

She felt the captain's arm circle around her waist and tensed. Behind her, he rested his free hand on the post above her head, and she could smell the faint, pleasant odor of tobacco when he spoke over her shoulder. "You must miss it terribly."

"No, I do not." She shook her head. "That's the curious thing. I don't miss it at all."

"Have you any idea how happy that makes me?"

She could not see his questioning gaze, but she imagined it, and leaned back until her head brushed against his wide, solid shoulder. "Tell me why does that make you happy? Isn't it a pitiful thing not to miss your family?"

"Well I have come to find, Miss Scott, we can choose to be happy wherever we hang our hats."

"Hmm. Well said, or bonnet you mean?"

He chuckled and relented, "Or bonnet. When family is far away, we make our own."

"Yes," Julia agreed. She thought him lucky to have a whole company of men at his disposal. "Your ship is your family, one would imagine."

"Oh, no," he said with a quiet laugh, surprising her. "There is no occasion for me to be family-like aboard a naval ship. That is for the crew and their companies. A captain's post is a lonely one."

"You set yourself apart then?"

"Yes. I don't have the comfort of being familiar with the men that sail with me. It wouldn't be proper or effectual."

Julia found a single blazing star and stared at it until she could place it in a constellation she did not know. She turned to face him, settling her back against the veranda's solid post. "So who is your family while you're away?" She almost felt sorry for the man, whose face now hovered so close she could see into his eyes despite the night.

"I have a few good friends, acquaintances on this island, and others."

"A few good friends are nothing to sneeze at," she reprimanded him.

He smiled and his teeth glimmered in the darkness. "You have made that abundantly true," he whispered.

Julia felt that she should smile, but his nearness made her nervous. Her heart tripped along like a faltering pony, while her palms grew damp with anxiety. He studied her in the shadows, and his gaze drifted from her eyes across her cheeks and to her mouth. "Captain Dewey," she breathed, afraid the quivering in her chest might find its way out with the words, "we should go back inside."

He moved, slowly, running a warm hand down her arm until it closed around her fingers. "You're right, Miss Scott," he said, not moving one little bit away, "they'll wonder what we are about." He smiled wider again then it dissipated as he moved his head to hers until their mouths touched. He skimmed his lips across hers, and stopped to rest them on her cheek.

Julia's pulse hummed like a mosquito in her ears. She could no longer hear insects chirping in the dark or the sound of the wind whipping up the ridge and over the trees past the grounds. Her fingers involuntarily squeezed the captain's hand. He laughed softly in his throat and moved way, so quickly that she gasped a bit. It made her feel fragile and foolish, but he only chuckled again. He never let go of her fingers, but led her back into the house and to the drawing room, where he stood by her side until it was time for all of the guests to retire.

CHAPTER SIX

"Well," said Lady Gordon, "don't you look splendid?" Julia turned this way and that, examining herself in the long looking glass. She felt at the same time spoiled and overcome with gratitude.

"I should not accept it," she murmured. The lavender gown made her eyes glow. They appeared more blue than green and did not look so queer in her pale face against her dark curls.

"Of course, you should!" Lady Gordon scolded. "There's nothing wrong with accepting gifts from your favorite uncle."

"My uncle I haven't seen in almost eight years." Julia stood tall and studied the round puffed sleeves on her shoulders.

"A pair of morning dresses and a delicious ivory ball gown is not such an extravagance." Lady Gordon raised a fist of fluttering ribbons in salmon and cream and held them just over Julia's shoulder. "He's more than happy to see to your needs. Besides, he doesn't have his own daughters and no wife either. These would match fine, would they not?"

Julia nodded. The long ribbons danced about her shoulder and her neck. She loved the lavender gown. It made her seem elegant.

"You look divine," Lady Gordon said to Julia's reflection. From behind her, she gave Julia a small embrace. "Everyone already thinks so, so you might as well enjoy your welcome."

The woman stopped speaking suddenly and turned her head to examine her own features in the looking glass. "You should enjoy your age, too," she added with a frown.

Julia chuckled. "You are too generous with your compliments."

The seamstress sitting quietly by the sun lit window rose from her seat. Her mouth was full of pins. She looked ready to poke Julia from head to toe.

After taking careful measurements and sewing a few darts here and there, the seamstress helped her back into her clothes. She escaped and waited at the shop door for her chaperone, watching a sluggish parade of carts and old carriages ramble up and down the sandy streets. It amused her that so much of home's customs and habits were in full effect here, even though that place was far away on what seemed the other side of the world.

Julia put her forehead to the pane to watch a lime green lizard sunning himself on the sill. The glass was blurred, not quite clear enough to see the fine details she knew were there. A dark, round shadow superimposed itself over the glass, and she jumped back. The shadow was a dark, laughing face. She heard him through the window and pursed her lips in condemnation, whether or not he could see her. His silhouette moved to the door, and he pushed it open, looking up when the bell jingled. "They'll be rushing out to dress you next," Julia warned.

Mr. Greenway stopped mid-stride into the dressmakers. He scanned the shelves of fabric and rolls of ribbon festooning the shop like a bridal party. "Whatever are you doing in here?" He turned to Julia, hands on hips.

"I should ask you the same. Are you buying more gowns for your victims?"

"Victims?" He reared back, raising a brow in question. "You hardly look the victim."

"I'm not. I've come to Falmouth with Lady Gordon to order more options for my wardrobe."

"Aren't you lucky?" Greenway's mouth curled into its familiar, wry grin. "I see your brother has sent you some money at last."

Julia frowned darkly. He had not, but enough time had passed, she guessed, for him to have received her letters. "My uncle has been so kind."

"Well," said Greenway, "I rather think that's more appropriate considering he's your godfather."

"Yes," she nodded, "and thank you for seeing to my recovery here."

"You've thanked me already."

"I can't help but feel it isn't enough." She smiled at him, gratitude blossoming out of her heart and warming her from head to toe. "It is good to see you."

"You've been bored," he guessed.

"Oh, it's not true! I've studied the Leewards you know, like you suggested, and I'm learning my way around the garden. We just had a dinner party three nights ago with company from all over the island."

"Yes, so I have heard." said Greenway in a particular tone.

"You knew about it?"

"It's Sir Henry, my dear. When he has a party, it gives people something to talk about."

"It wasn't that thrilling," Julia promised. She frowned. Her opinion did not include Captain Dewey's stolen kisses, but she could not own up to that.

Greenway laughed at her. "You're not so easily impressed, are you?"

"I'm not so good with names," she confessed. "Oh, but Captain Dewey you know of course," she eyed Greenway directly to check his memory.

He made a face like he'd licked a lemon. "Who can forget our illustrious captain? Has he apologized for tossing you overboard?"

"Now, be fair. He didn't know I was who I claimed to be."

"I did." Greenway shrugged, nonchalant. "I'm happy to see he has found extra time to spend ashore with his busy career." A streaming ray of sunlight found its way through the windows to hit the hard, polished floor. Greenway stirred at it with his boot.

"He's shown me around the harbor, yes," Julia admitted. "He likes to read your kind of books, too."

"Does he now?" Greenway's voice was kind but disbelieving.

"He does," Julia said with a little laugh.

They eyed one another. Greenway looked doubtful, and it made her giggle.

"Mr. Greenway," said Lady Gordon with surprise. She crossed the room in three steps and held out her hand. "I am so happy to see you again."

"You have missed me loitering about your home?"

"Of course we have. Have we not, Miss Scott?"

Julia grinned and smiled sincerely. "We have to be sure."

"Are you up to more of your good deeds?" queried Lady Gordon. "Are you here to buy a new gown or bonnet for another damsel in distress?"

When Greenway smiled mysteriously, Julia felt a bolt of jealousy she instantly chided herself for. "I am not shopping," he said. "I deny any such insinuation."

Lady Gordon chuckled. "Then we are just lucky to cross paths today."

"It is not chance so much," he said. "I recognized your carriage from the street, and thought I would pay respects to my favorite cousin."

"They're always welcome." The lady dropped a polite, unnecessary curtsey. Julia did the same when he doffed his hat and looked toward the door. "I must take my leave," he said, more to himself than the ladies.

"Back to business?" Julia teased.

He glanced down at his elegant trousers. "Business, yes." He gave her a secretive grin she couldn't interpret, but it made her smile anyway.

"Good day, Mr. Greenway," she called as he left. Lady Gordon gave a little wave.

"Until next time," he called back over his shoulder.

Surprised at a surge of wistfulness stirring in her heart, Julia hoped next time would be soon.

THE LAST PERSON SHE expected to see one week later was Captain Dewey. He stood waiting for her in the drawing room after breakfast.

"Captain," Julia said in surprise, "I thought you were at sea."

"So I was," he admitted. "I'm just ashore for the day."

"You have more business?"

"Not this time." He smiled as if he knew something she didn't.

"What is it?"

"It's nothing," he laughed. "Truly, there is a problem with the mainmast, and I wanted it repaired well and proper." He glanced out the window at fast moving clouds tumbling over one another in the cerulean sky. "One never knows when the weather will turn."

"Yes," Julia agreed. "Yesterday's rain shower was sudden and violent. I'm glad it didn't last. Besides, I'm of the opinion it's better to be prepared than to be caught unawares."

He smiled at her again so intently, she shifted her gaze to the floor. "I've spoken with Lady Gordon just now," he said, drawing her attention. "She thinks it's a fine day for me to take you for a row?"

"A row?" Julia scrunched her forehead.

"Out on the lagoon? I thought we could make a day of it, before it gets too hot anyway."

"Ah." Julia bit her lip.

"The water's clear, and we'll have no interruptions," Captain Dewey promised.

"How can I refuse that?" Julia pressed her lips together in a smile and hurried out for her new bonnet and parasol from one of the shops in Falmouth. They walked arm in arm down the long path to the harbor and across the quay to a small lagoon. Captain Dewey left her under the shade of tall, spidery mangrove tree while he pushed a small dinghy to the edge of the water. He motioned for her to come, and she ploughed through thick heavy sand, amused at how it filled up the cracks between her feet and high soled shoes.

"I'll be shaking sand from my stockings for weeks," she complained with a teasing grin.

"That's the fun of it." Dewey reached for her hand and helped her into the wobbly craft. She took her seat gingerly, so as not to toss them both into the shallow water. It was beautiful; bluer than the brightest sapphire.

Captain Dewey took the oars and rowed them out into deeper water. It shifted from blue to emerald green, and then to the brightest navy. She could no longer see the rocky bottom with its chunks of dark coral.

"It's safe here in the harbor?" she wondered. Schools of silver fish flashed by.

"Of course it is, and you're with me."

Balancing the parasol against her shoulder, Julia lifted her chin to look at him from beneath the brim of her bonnet. "I'm not worried, Captain Dewey. I wouldn't have agreed to this adventure if I didn't think I'd make it through."

He laughed at her, and she noticed the way the sun hit his sharp cheekbones and lit up his brown eyes. He'd removed his blue coat and worked only in his white trousers, linen shirt, and dark waistcoat. It looked cooler, and he looked more natural.

"Have you spoken with your uncle?" Dewey said, breaking the pleasant silence between them.

"Not exactly," she admitted. "Of course you would know he is not yet returned. He's sent word to Sir Henry and his wife, and they insist I remain with them until he returns to English Harbor."

"He's quite busy, one would expect."

"Yes, I know," Julia admitted, "but I have no intention of getting in his way. He wrote that he has room enough and looks forward to my company. I won't be alone in his house either, for Lady Gordon tells me he keeps a butler and house-keeper who keep things in order when he's at sea.

"Hmm." Captain Dewey's remark sounded more of interest than approval. He let the dinghy ride a mild current on its own accord, resting his hands on the ends of the oars. His dark hat, worn athwartships, or side to side, sat low on his forehead, but not so low she could not see his appraising stare. "Your eyes are as turquoise as the tide. I've never seen such a peculiar shade of blue and green, except here in the Indies." He smiled at her.

Julia glanced around at the sapphire waves lapping gently around them. "Thank you." She could think of nothing more to say. His flattery surprised her. While growing up, Hiram had teased her endlessly that she clearly could not make up her mind. Caroline had called them startling and odd.

Captain Dewey cocked his head, eyeing her from the side of his face, his lips pursed. "You have not received a great many compliments in your life, or else you don't believe me." He gave her a questioning stare.

Julia contemplated how much she should confess. In a voice subdued by an ache in her chest she said, "Not a great many, no. I daresay, I haven't had the opportunity to receive them living with my stepmother in the country."

"You never went to London or perhaps Bath for recreation?"

Julia shook her head. "No, never."

"What a shame," said the captain, "but I understand it better now."

"Understand what?"

"Why you haven't been swept away by some eager, young buck."

The imagery of his words caused Julia to burst out in laughter. "No, I have not been swept away by anyone or anything. Only... circumstance I'd suppose."

"You mean how your family has sent you to live with the admiral."

"Yes."

"How long do you intend to stay?"

That was a question that Julia had asked herself often. "I do not know. Admiral Hammond is my godfather and my own parents are dead, God rest their souls."

"Lady Gordon tells me he sounds full of joy to have family at last in the Indies, and looks forward to seeing you again."

"I hope he will enjoy the company."

Dewey grinned. "I know I do." He gazed too long at her, and Julia felt herself blush. She shook her head to shake away his compliments.

"I am fully committed to not be in his way or underfoot," she promised. "I'll make myself useful at his home, and with Lady Gordon, too."

"She's grown fond of you." Dewey looked over his shoulder toward the shore as if contemplating whether or not they should return.

Even with the parasol overhead, Julia could feel the heat working its way past her protective barriers. Perspiration trickled down her hips and rolled over her thighs. She'd be soaked through before too long, and it might show. She fanned herself with her fingers to move the air along, but Dewey had begun to stroke again, moving the little craft back toward the middle of the bay and its dark water.

"Lady Gordon is my newest and best friend. I'm happy to come to Antigua, but I shouldn't worry her or give her cause to call the physician again. We should get out of this boiling sun."

"Of course," Dewey said. He seemed disconcerted for a moment, but in the next he hoisted the oars once more and spun them about with ease.

"How long have you been captain of the *Triumph*?" Julia wondered.

He smiled again. "Two years. I was lieutenant before that, and graduated from midshipman aboard the *Sophie*. You have heard of her?"

Julia shook her head she had not.

Captain Dewey grinned. "She's little but water tight and moves at a clipper's pace."

"You sound like you miss her so."

"I do," he said happily, "but not too much. She's running post in the Channel, but Bonaparte's men won't catch her. The *Triumph* is the ship for me. I worked too long and hard for my promotions."

"You're so young," Julia said with feeling. "You're one of the youngest captains I've seen." Her observation made the captain beam. He looked boyish.

"Some would say my connections are the reason, but I've a good record and a clean crew. We took a little French brig just last month, not long before we discovered you and Greenway bobbing along."

At the reminder of her previous adventure, Julia wrinkled her nose. "You saved us from certain death, Captain Dewey." Before she could go on, he winked at her and gave her his funny stare again. It made her stomach flip flop and left her tongue tied.

"You've saved me," he said in a low, earnest tone. It was the timbre he'd used on the veranda at Sir Henry's dinner party, when he whispered in her ear and kissed her.

She flushed at the recollection, and wondered if she should feel ashamed. What she had allowed was nothing short of scandalous. "How have I saved you?" she asked quietly.

"Why, from loneliness of course. I'm without family here as you know." He smiled at her, and took another stroked pushing them closer to the shore. "You must know you are far better company than the fo'c'sle."

Julia smiled. "You love your men, you told me so."

"Of course I love them, for their purpose and effort. They make me look capable in my post," he jested.

She chuckled at him this time. "Well, what's not to love about anyone who makes us look capable?"

"Exactly," he said, "you understand me completely."

CHAPTER SEVEN

Lady Gordon held her by the elbows, not two days later, unconcerned Julia was half-dressed in her shift and her hair undone from its long braid. "I have news," Lady Gordon said. She sounded out of breath like she'd run to the room.

"It's good I hope," Julia replied. The interruption left her somewhat unsettled.

"It is, but it's not new news, it's old news. I wanted to be sure it would not be cancelled so you weren't disappointed."

"It takes a great deal to disappoint me," promised Julia.

"Well, then," said Lady Gordon, satisfied, "there will be an officers' ball before the rains come, after all."

"Is there usually?"

"Oh yes! We make our own merry here. Any excuse will do." Lady Gordon reached for Julia's hands. "That's what moved me to visit the dressmakers, but I wanted to make sure you were prepared as well."

Julia thought of the embroidered white muslin gown that had not yet arrived. "You do think it will be finished on time?"

"I'm told it's done," the lady said with excitement. "Your gown and my gown, too. They're completely finished and will be here by tomorrow. I've been promised it, and I expect everyone I deal with to keep their promises." She gave Julia's hand a squeeze. "You will come, won't you? Sir Henry and I will act as chaperones."

"Of course I will," breathed Julia with excitement.

"Your poor uncle," the lady crooned, "won't he be sorry to miss it. I'm afraid I am getting ahead with all his fun."

"I doubt Uncle Richard will have many regrets missing a ball."

"I'm not sure about that," said Lady Gordon. "He will miss out on your official introduction, although you've met most of my friends and the ladies of our little congregation." She referred to the island's nearby white stone church with its stunted steeple.

"If he approves of it, I'm happy to go."

"And well you should," replied Lady Gordon. "I'm sure a certain Captain we know will make an appearance. Why, it's like a second coming out."

Julia tried not to flush. "If he is ashore, I would not be surprised." She did not tell her friend she had never had a coming out to start with, because of her father's sudden death and Caroline's harsh decisions about their future.

"Now, don't play coy. He's not spent this much time in English Harbor all for business."

Julia smiled again, warmth tinging her cheeks. She enjoyed his attentions, she could not deny. To dance with him would be a pleasant way to spend an evening.

"Mr. Greenway has already inquired of your situation."

"Has he? How kind."

"He's a gentleman," said Lady Gordon. "He heard about the ball, and his first thought was you should have something to wear and be happy to attend."

"I will be happy to go," said Julia with determination. The thought that Mr. Greenway might also be there made her happier still. "He knows I have something to wear. He discovered us ordering gowns."

Lady Gordon laughed. "Well, I'm not usually happy to wile away my every evening with my husband's associates, but with you and my own dear friends I think I can make the most of it."

Julia squeezed Lady Gordon's hands in return. "We will both make the most of it.

AFTER VISITING TWO ill sisters from the church as Lady Gordon's companion, Julia spent the day on the grounds, picking at flowers and dallying in the vegetable garden with its fascinating rows of peppers set apart from the sweet potatoes. She returned to the shade of the veranda with her sketch book in hand, but before she could settle in, a man on horseback clopped down the drive and dismounted before the house. She recognized Mr. Greenway at once, the narrow width of his shoulders and lean build, or maybe it was the way he moved. He seemed to bounce right off the chestnut as surely as he would have bounced up to mount it. Her spirits, dulled by the heat of the day, rose like a kite. She put down her pencil and watched his approach. He spied her as he sprang toward the stairs, and took off his hat as he raced up to the shaded portico.

"How are your lessons?" He did not ring the bell, but joined her in the corner cove, standing with his back to the sun, his arms at his side.

She tipped the drawing down so he could see it. "I've studied your birds and flowers as much as I could bear. I prefer to make my own books."

"With pictures?"

Julia frowned. "There's nothing wrong with drawings. All of the best books have illustrations."

Mr. Greenway grinned. "Is that so? Let me see your work."

Struck with shyness, Julia hesitated, but Greenway held out his hand so eagerly she could not refuse him. He thumbed through the pages, nodding to himself at each sketch. "You have a gift for drawing flora," he said decidedly. "You draw as well as you sing." His approval filled her with pleasure.

"Do you really think so?"

"Yes, I do. This however," he flinched and pivoted the book so she could see the rather bad sketch of a rabbit, "that's the silliest rat I've ever seen."

Julia burst into laughter. She put her fingers to her eyelids and dabbed at them. "That's not a rat," she confessed. "It's a rabbit."

Greenway grimaced. He shook his head in despair. "It's dreadful, my girl." He sighed. "You need to spend more time observing your subjects."

"He hopped away," Julia exclaimed. She arose from the long narrow bench she'd been resting on, just high enough to snatch her book away from Greenway's hands. He caught her by the wrist and pulled her to her feet.

"The flowers are well enough," he said, "but you need something that won't hop away. Come with me."

Julia looked around in concern. "I should tell Lady Gordon—"

"She won't mind. We won't leave the grounds. There's something better than rabbits or lizards I think you could capture quite well in your drawing book."

"Well, if you're certain." Julia smoothed down her gown with one hand, but didn't pull the other from Greenway's hold. It was nice to be close to him again. He made her feel comfortable and safe, and his conversation both amused her and put her at ease. That was, as long as he did not stand close or examine her too long with his rifle green gaze. He led her across the house and over the flat grounds with its sparse scattering of trees.

"Now that," he pointed upward, "is a breadfruit tree, and you should do well to learn to sketch its fruit."

"I know that's a breadfruit tree," Julia replied with disgust in her tone. "I told you I've studied your recommended foci for the Leewards."

"If you draw it, you won't forget it," he promised her.

She gazed heavenward as if he tried her patience but really she found it endearing he was so eager for her to know everything about her new home. They came to the crest of the hill from where the path dropped to the steep, sandy overlook. "I thought you told me not to come down to this spot."

"I told you not to wander down here alone," he corrected. His hand slid down her arm, and he grasped for her hand. A warm feeling of security moved through Julia along with a surge of affection.

They edged carefully down the slope, and she slipped once. It would have been a tumble if he hadn't snatched her around the waist. With her back snuggly to him, he lifted her back onto her toes. "Steady now," he warned.

She recovered and led him the rest of the way down. They stopped at the sandy rise and surveyed the view from east to west. "It's lovely," she sighed. The island curved around them from each side of their vantage point like butterfly wings. The sky shimmered with golden sunlight and reflected off the mirrored surface of the sea. "Blue as a peacock feather," Julia whispered. A steady breeze ruffled the palms and plant fronds growing along the hillside. She closed her eyes and let it blow through her thin muslin layers and across the back of her neck.

"You don't have a bonnet," Greenway said in the quiet. His voice sounded gruff but not scolding. "I just discovered it, and now you will be red as a plumrose before the ball."

"Oh!" Julia shaded her face with her hand. "I forgot it. You had me so curious I left my parasol on the veranda."

"Well with luck, everyone will admire your healthy color."

"Yes," she agreed. "No worries, and I happen to like a plumrose."

He laughed. She felt a motion behind her and felt his hat plop down firmly on the crown of her head. "There. That should salvage your complexion anyway."

"It's probably too late for that." Julia tore her gaze away from her favorite scene and looked over her shoulder to find Greenway's eyes inches from hers. Her mind stuttered a few steps, but she found her tongue and said, "I have two sunspots. See? Here." She pointed to the bridge of her nose, where one spot had popped up after the skin healed from her first burn. The other was just to the side, under her eye.

"What a shame," Greenway whispered. He stared as if captivated by the damage on her skin.

Julia laughed under her breath and stepped away. His nearness unnerved her. She knew what Captain Dewey would do if he stood so close. At the thought of the captain and his gentle attempts to kiss her again after their row in the harbor, she felt hot and uncomfortable.

What Greenway thought of her sudden flush she could not tell, but he stepped back and surveyed the view. "Do you see what I mean?" He changed the subject as easily as he changed his moods. "From there you see the harbor and ships, and across the way, open ocean. To our right is Falmouth and the rest is the distant horizon."

"Yes," Julia agreed. She turned her attention back to the distant border where sea met sky. Two shades of blues kissed and merged into one. "I could draw this. I hadn't thought of it before."

"I challenge you," Greenway dared, "but only with an escort. It will keep you busy until your uncle returns and puts you to work keeping his house."

Julia laughed. "I'd be too happy to, you must know."

"I'm sure you will find some way to be an asset even with help underfoot."

"I do hope so." Julia sighed. She closed her eyes and concentrated on the breeze again. "I suppose I should be flattered you're concerned I keep busy enough."

"Idle hands are the devil's workshop," Greenway quipped.

She laughed. "I have not been idle, I promise."

"So I have heard."

She peered at him from the corners of her eyes, as he'd moved to stand beside her. "From whom, may I ask?"

"Only a mutual friend. You and the *Triumph's* captain are the talk of town."

"Captain Dewey?" Julia inhaled sharply. "He calls on Sir Henry on occasion, and he's walked me around the island. Oh, well, yes, there was an adventure on the lagoon," she confided. She grinned. "He took me for a row in the lagoon beyond the harbor.

"Is that so?" Greenway said wryly. "Did he think you missed being adrift?"

Julia's hand flitted to her mouth to keep from laughing. "He was only trying to entertain me. It was kind of him really."

"I suppose," Greenway admitted grudgingly. "Although I'm not sure what business he would have with Sir Henry. I would think the Navy would be on his list of commitments, or perhaps the Admiral."

"If he were here," Julia said.

Greenway said nothing. Julia gazed out over the water at tall masted ships that looked miniature from her vantage point. "I think you're right, I should sketch this scene. If I take my time it could be a handsome piece."

"You will need watercolors," Greenway murmured. He patted her head, still covered with his hat that smelled faintly of sun and tar and something male and pleasant.

"I can't do a watercolor," she confessed. "Surely you know. I'm no good at watercolor, or netting, or the pianoforte, or much else I should be."

"You make a fine list of your shortcomings," Greenway observed. "I rather think you should focus on your abilities."

"There aren't many. It's true."

"How about your voice? Why don't you sing for us at the ball?"

Heat rushed to Julia's cheeks making them so warm she felt dizzy. "I've never sung for more than a few people at a time. I'd feel so nervous, so put on display."

"You sang for an island of natives," Greenway reminded her.

"That was different. They didn't understand a word of it, and you didn't give me any choice in the matter."

"You don't need to speak the same language to understand a song."

"Well said," Julia admitted. "Still... I could not." She elbowed him, and he grabbed his side as if it pained him much more than it could have. "How did you hear of the ball? Are you coming then? Will you be ashore?"

"So many questions," Greenway teased. "I heard of it from Lady Morland in the apothecary's shop and received my invitation yesterday morning."

"You will be there?"

"I plan to make an appearance. I'll dance with you if you sing."

Julia laughed. "I will not sing."

Greenway's mouth curled up in a sinister grin, and he narrowed his eyes.

Julia poked him with her elbow again. "Don't you dare think of volunteering me."

He put a hand to his chin, chastised. "I must leave by the next morning. Business you know." He glanced out to sea.

"Do come," Julia pleaded. "I will dance with you if you come, but you must promise not to make me sing."

"I never make a vow I can't keep," said Greenway. He lifted his hat from Julia's head and took her arm to lead her back up toward the grounds. "Now, I have business with Sir Henry about the dockyard, and you have given me your word you will sometime sketch the view from the knoll. I expect you to stay occupied with your studies until the ball."

"Yes, sir." Julia raised her hand to her forehead in a mock salute. He led her back up to the house joking about her attempts to draw the island's vermin, and they went in together just in time for tea.

THE NIGHT BEFORE THE ball Julia tossed restlessly in her bed. The heat seemed oppressive as ever. For some reason the breeze decided to bypass its usual route from the shore, up the ridge, and around the Gordon's house. The air felt still. She sat up, kicked off her thin blanket, and pulled her nightdress up to her thighs. All she could think of were the cool, damp rooms of Netley Hall, and how relaxing it could be under the shade of a favorite oak tree.

Julia had been an innocent captive in her own home, but she was now a young woman free of her family's restraints on the other side of the equator. Under Lady Gordon's lenient guidance, she was free to do what she pleased for the most part. Like kiss the captain of a ship of the line.

Her heart filled with shame should Mr. Greenway ever know she had let someone kiss her. And Papa. Even Hiram. Mr. Greenway may have seen her improperly attired and in various stages of disgrace, but he had never influenced her to the point she would lower her morals for shallow reasons. There was no way to make him understand that Captain Dewey made her feel special and important. Besides, it had been an accident really, that she had kissed him back at all. He had initiated it after all, and her curiosity had won. His handsomeness was stirring to look upon.

Flopping back down on fluffed feather pillows, she plucked idly at the hem of her lightweight chemise. The ball would be more enjoyable if Mr. Greenway attended. She wouldn't feel so tense and uncomfortable with all eyes upon her, the admiral's niece. Why at home she was hardly noticeable, just a daughter of a gentleman with a modest living, but in the Indies her connections seemed to raise her footing in society somewhat. At least with Sir Henry and Captain Dewey. She didn't expect Mr. Greenway would care one way or the other who her connections were in the Leewards. He hadn't even known her true identity until after his rescue. A good heart, that one, she decided.

Much like her papa, her uncle, and the truly good men she had known in her life, George Henry Greenway had a good heart despite whatever mischief he had been up to with the nasty lot of pirates. She was lucky fate had tossed them together in turmoil. They were so alike in some ways, teasing and willful, it was sure they would end up the best of friends when it all was said and done.

THE COURTHOUSE ON THE far side of the island stood as the designated assembly hall for special occasions. The ball, thrown by the social elite of the island, invited all those who lived and contributed to the colony's wealth and security.

Julia felt honored to be invited even if she was a guest of Sir Henry and his wife. He was a quiet, kind man who had little to say beyond polite greetings and inquiries into her health, but she was fond of him if only because he was married to Lady Gordon, who was the most fun and accomplished lady she'd ever been happy to consort with.

They linked arms like best friends as the carriage bounced roughly over the rolling hills. She might have been more than ten years her senior, but Julia felt Lady Gordon a handsome friend and believed her every word except when she would go on about her ward's looks.

"Let me see it," she begged, making Julia turn her head and show the long ostrich feather pinned tightly into her coiled hair. "It's lovely," Lady Gordon promised her. "It dances and sways with the slightest turn of your chin."

Julia thanked her. She had been surprised to see the young woman look back at her from the looking glass. The long white gown in the French style she so favored, was embroidered with rosettes around the hem. Lady Gordon's maid had woven blue ribbons into Julia's thin braids, before coiling them perfectly centered on her crown. She then pinned in the feather, a gift from her hostess. With curls framing her face from forehead to cheek, and the little drop pearl earrings Lady Gordon had loaned her, Julia felt pretty indeed. So much so, the image of Caroline came unbidden into her mind. Her stepmother's sharp features and eternal frown forced Julia's opinion of herself back down where it belonged. Uncle Richard would return before long, and she would be set up as a spinster relative, no longer welcome in her English home, sent to be dealt with by an old bachelor with more income and patience. Tonight would be her last celebration of youth and freedom.

"Here we are," cried Lady Gordon, more excited than a married chaperone should be. She squeezed Julia's hand. "I'm so excited for you, Miss Scott. You will meet everyone now."

"You must call me Julia."

Lady Gordon smiled in satisfaction, and Julia studied the layer of powder dusting the lady's face and chin. She took a deep breath, and when the carriage door opened, waited for Sir Henry and his wife to descend, half hoping to be half-forgotten in the throng.

They were whisked indoors by liveried footmen who looked uncomfortable in their clothes and less excited than the attendees flocking toward the courthouse doors. Everyone on the island seemed to be dressed in their finest attire. It was all very proper, just as a seasonal ball in Town would be, or even the assembly rooms in Bath as she'd often imagined.

After a formal introduction which made Julia's knees quiver, they merged with the growing crowd in the large room to be used as a ballroom. It glittered with candlelight and crystals. Bouquets of jasmine made the billowing breeze smell inviting. She was hardly oriented to her surroundings when the first dance was called and before she could paste a smile of contentment on her face, Captain Dewey appeared from out of the crowd and bowed deeply.

"Captain!" she said with pleasure. "You have come after all."

"I gave my word I would make every effort to be ashore. We can't have you standing idly about like a wallflower." His joke made her blush. "You have promised me the first two dances. You haven't forgotten, have you?"

"Of course I remember." Julia couldn't help but smile. Did he think she would forget him so easily?

"Sir Henry," Dewey said to her chaperones, "and Lady Gordon." He bowed deeply and inquired of their health as the musicians began to tweak their instruments. Another admirer of the general's party joined their little throng. Already anxious and excited, Julia's heart soared when she realized it was Greenway. He took Lady Gordon's hand and exchanged pleasantries, then moved a step down the line to Julia.

"I hardly recognized you," he confessed, appraising her from head to toe with intensity.

"Did you not? I knew her at once," Captain Dewey declared, moving closer to Julia's side.

"With that ridiculous turkey feather bobbing up and down, I thought a bird was loose in the room."

Julia pursed her lips and thwacked Greenway on the chest with the tip of her folded fan. "It's an ostrich feather, and you should know, seeing as your ships probably supply them to the entire Leewards."

Greenway grinned, although she already knew he teased her. His eyes were shadowed in the candlelight, so mossy and dark they looked like onyx stones. "I thought I should ask for the first dance, before all of your admirers commit you for the evening."

Julia laughed. "What admirers?" She looked around the room. All of the other men near her age were preoccupied with conversations or lining up on the floor to dance. A few caught her eye, but she assumed they were taking inventory of the room and who was available.

Greenway offered his hand, but Captain Dewey cut him off. "I'm sorry, dear fellow," said Dewey, "but she's promised me the first two dances. You'll have to wait."

The captain pressed the small of Julia's back so firmly she had to take a step to keep her balance. She chuckled, not because Greenway looked irritated, but because the captain made himself sound older than Greenway, and he was not.

He shot her a look of dismay and then turned to Lady Gordon without another word. Julia's heart flinched for him. Not that he was embarrassed, because nothing ruffled Mr. Greenway, but because he might think she did not want to dance with him. Her heart told her she very much did. They had experienced so many other things together, why not a West Indies ball? She loved the newness of her life, and he liked to share in her discoveries.

Before she could promise him a dance, Captain Dewey led her out onto the floor with a strong arm and positioned her on the proper side for the dance that had been called. She curtseyed, and he bowed, and then she forgot what she should be thinking as she mentally counted the steps she'd had so little opportunity to execute. She flushed with mild embarrassment when she noticed Captain Dewey following her every movement. It was difficult to pay him much attention while she watched the other ladies around her dance, following their lead as much as she dared and watching the other gentlemen.

Captain Dewey moved smoothly. One could not tell he spent most of his time aboard a swaying pile of timber. He looked most serious, eyes glimmering in the soft lighting and hand gripping her with a softness that made her feel fragile. When they came toe to toe, she smiled faintly, and he moved his head too near. She stepped back involuntarily, stumbling on the hem of her gown.

On the final chords of the elementary country dance, he crossed the space between them in one eager stride, bringing both of her hands up to his chin. "You look ravishing," he whispered.

Julia smiled. His enthusiastic compliment made her heart swell. His attentions now became very clear, and she realized for the first time how intense they were, so much so he would make a scene in front of others. Her gaze swept past his handsome face to Lady Gordon who watched them with a pleased grin. Mr. Greenway stood beside her, arms folded across his chest, a frown filling his face.

She danced with the captain a second time, and tried modestly to avoid his penetrating stare. His meaningful attendance made her heart flutter. Afterward, before she could join her chaperones and Mr. Greenway, another officer asked for her company. Captain Dewey reluctantly set her arm free.

With time, the steps became more familiar, and her mind worked less hard to make polite conversation. She smiled back when her kind partners smiled, and answered the brief, probing questions with simple replies. There were compliments of every kind, and she reckoned before the evening was through her head would be filled with her own self-importance. No one had made such a fuss over her less than ivory complexion before, nor her odd eye color. Here, along the equator, it matched the sea and seemed to be tolerable.

Captain Dewey found her before she could worry who would escort her to supper, and along with Sir Henry and Lady Gordon they joined the line of hungry dancers who discovered long tables heaped with food and sweets. She only took one cup of punch, fearing her giddiness combined with anything more would make her act foolish. The captain's accolades did not help. By the time she'd refreshed herself with Lady Gordon and returned to the ballroom, the candles stood at half their earlier height. The air felt humid and smelled musky and of alcohol.

She chatted with Lady Gordon and her circle of allies. Only one mentioned Captain Dewey's obvious attachment. Julia smiled the observation away without a word. The captain was a man of passion, it was clear. He was young and, for some reason, fancied an orphan with a poorly maintained complexion and peculiar eyes.

A familiar presence interrupted her deliberations. Over her shoulder, standing back in the shadows, Mr. Greenway reclined against a column with a potted palm beside him. Its fronds blocked a complete and open view of the ballroom, but he could see enough to satisfy himself or so it appeared. Because of the dimming candles, she wasn't sure if he watched her or the dancers and their reel. As she studied him appraising the room, he took a step near her, his features revealing nothing in the pool of light that fell over his face. Before he could speak, she asked anxiously, "Have you decided to dance with me after all?"

Greenway frowned. "Of course I have not. You've expended yourself enough for one evening. How do you find the strength to still be on your feet?"

She smiled, although a little pang twisted in her heart. "I'd be mortified if you refused me when it's improper and unseemly for me to mention it, but it's only you Mr. Greenway, so I will not let it trouble me."

"Oh, you will not?" He moved closer until they were side by side, but did not look at her again. He watched the reel instead. "If I thought it would be any source of humiliation, I would not have said it so."

"Don't you like to dance? I noticed you asked every young widow that I know and the two sisters who live around the cove in the pink stone house."

"Widows and spinsters," Greenway said in a dull tone, "that's my specialty."

Julia giggled. She spotted Captain Dewey across the room engaged in a turbulent conversation with a lieutenant of another ship, and angled herself so he would not notice her catching her breath.

"I do not understand why you say such things," she scolded Greenway. "Everyone knows there's a shortage of young ladies in the West Indies. I'm not conceited enough to think I've turned everyone's head."

"Are you certain?" her companion remarked.

She narrowed her eyes and pressed her lips together. "Do you find me vain?"

"I do not."

"Then why are you so sour this evening, especially of all nights?"

Greenway said nothing for a pause, and Julia wondered why it made her heart pick up its pace. His hesitation gave her some anxiety.

"To be frank, Miss Scott, I'd hoped to have the pleasure of a dance before I take my leave, but I did not expect to find you committed to the first two dances."

"Oh," said Julia. "It was the captain's idea, you must know. He asked me, and I had no reason to refuse."

"Did you not?" Greenway gave her a peculiar stare, his brows raised with sincere interest.

She shook her head. "No. Not that I know. Was it wrong?" She lowered her voice and leaned over close to him so he would hear her. "Do you think it was improper?"

"Well," said Greenway, crossing his arms over his chest. "What would your stepmother say?"

Julia flinched. "Caroline? Why she would... Why she would have found a reason to keep me home, so it doesn't really matter at all, does it?" She could not help but grit her teeth. Thinking of Caroline raised bitter feelings in her gut that made her feel ill.

Greenway whispered in her ear, "I'd like to have a word with you." He turned to one of the doors, his arm outstretched behind his back. Surprised, but brimming with curiosity, Julia slipped a bare hand into his grip. She had removed her gloves because they stifled her fingers and made her palms perspire. Mr. Greenway's rough hand clasped hers, and he led her out of the ballroom and down a wide hall before letting go. They strolled quickly arm in arm toward a door at the far end of the wing, and then onto a balcony that looked out over the white square buildings lining the street for as far as she could see into the night. There was very little moonlight, but the stars appeared numberless. They made the heavens look like blinking fireflies on black canvas.

Mr. Greenway stopped at the carved terrace rail and looked down into the street. It was much higher than Julia anticipated, and her examination of it made her dizzy. She stepped back, bumped into Greenway, and he dropped her arm but slid down and caught up her hand again. The familiarity of his touch made her tremble, and she wondered why it would trouble her so. From his blank expression, it was more natural than anything else. She had cried in his lap after all, and while he was improperly attired at that.

Greenway cleared his throat like he would speak, but relaxed instead, and the music from the ballroom drifted out and wrapped itself around them. The breeze flapped the potted plants lined up like soldiers every few paces along the balcony. Julia rested her free arm on the rail and leaned over it again to see if she could look below at carriages lining up for departing guests without the world spinning. "This is much better than dancing," she said.

Greenway squeezed her hand. It felt warm and safe. When he finally spoke his voice was hushed. "I'm happy you think so, but I'm sure I will have regrets tomorrow."

"Don't regret not dancing with me. You still have your toes, so be thankful for it." Although she could not bring herself to stare at him directly because of his contemplative mood, she saw him smile to himself.

"You are not too terrible a dancer."

Julia chuckled. "I'm sure there is an officer or two inside that might disagree."

"An officer, yes, that is what I wished to speak to you about."

Julia nerves tightened with apprehension. Mr. Greenway noticed everything. "You mean Captain Dewey, I assume?"

"Of course." Greenway sounded wry. "I'm reluctant to leave the Leewards for a time with your uncle unable to watch over you."

"Sir Henry and Lady Gordon are good chaperones, are they not?" Julia could not keep the challenge out of her voice. She hadn't behaved that disgracefully, had she?

"They are well enough, but you need the guidance and protection of family."

"It won't be long, less than a fortnight now, according to his last letter."

"Still, I question whether or not I should stay."

A part of Julia was pleased at the idea of Greenway staying, but she could not say so, not when he had done so much for her already. "You must go. You have business, or your mysterious affairs, and I could be no safer than I already am."

"Of that, I'm not so sure."

"What do you mean?"

"I mean, Captain Dewey." His voice changed from soft to cold when he said the officer's name.

"Captain Dewey would do me no harm," Julia returned. "He's very kind and attentive, and has made me feel welcome and accepted."

"Has he now?"

"Why do you always ask me questions when you already know the answer?" Julia stomped her foot but restrained herself from giving him a kick in the shins.

"It's only, Miss Scott—"

"Oh for heaven's sake, you must call me Julia. After all we are far beyond an acquaintanceship now I should say."

"If you say so, but you know I cannot. It'd hardly be proper."

Julia almost snorted. There had been nothing proper between them from the start. "It's only what?" she inquired. "If you have concerns I wish to hear them."

He exhaled sharply and turned to her, with his face close and expression stern. "Captain Dewey is an ambitious man. He made lieutenant when he was sixteen. He was commander within a short period afterward, and earned his captain's epaulettes not three years ago."

"Is there something wrong with knowing what you want?"

Greenway's look became a frown again, as it seemed to do more often than not of late. "Yes," he replied slowly. "There is something wrong with wanting something for the wrong reason, for selfish purposes."

"What do you mean?"

He gazed at her in earnest. "I mean only that his interest in you is avariciousness. He has made it known to anyone who sails the West Indies that he will be admiral someday."

Julia felt her jaw drop. She was insulted, angry, and confused at the same time.

"He covets your uncle's position and will do anything to make his next rank and earn his next ship of the line."

"Are you saying he does not really like me? That he is using me to get close to my uncle?"

"Yes," answered Greenway, his stare unflinching. "I am saying exactly that."

"Oh!" Julia shook her hand from Greenway's grasp and stepped back. She took a deep breath as words tumbled into order from her horrified thoughts. "How can you say such things? Captain Dewey saved our lives. He has gone out of his way to see that I adjust to this new home and has done nothing avaricious or untoward."

Her heart lurched again, but this time at her little lie. Captain Dewey had kissed her, but she could not admit it to Greenway now. He was trying to rescue her again and in the worst possible way. Calling out another gentleman would not end well.

Greenway did not appear to be surprised at her outburst, nor did he drop his probing gaze. "I find I am invested in you, Miss Scott. Touching death's door with someone in kind, has a way of forming attachments that are rarely broken."

Julia bit her lip hard, trying to sort out what she could properly say and do. "I appreciate your concern, truly I do, but you have no right interjecting yourself into my personal affairs. It's wrong to speak ill of someone of such upstanding character. He means well. I know he does."

"It's for your own good," Greenway retorted, voice rising.

"I'm old enough to know my own good," Julia cried. "I've managed myself thus far, and I'll see to my own affairs, thank you very much."

"Don't be a fool," he snapped. "You believe every word that comes out of any mouth."

"I don't believe yours! You're just trying to—Well, you're as critical and suspicious as Caroline, and I won't... I won't stand here and listen to such cruel nonsense."

Greenway pierced her with a disappointed gaze, waiting for her to say more or relent, but she would do neither. She stomped her foot again and fled from the balcony, rounding the corner of the door so sharply she hit her shoulder and cried out.

"I'm sorry we did not dance, then. You are a vision in white." The wind carried along Greenway's parting words. Julia put her hands over her ears and ran back to the shadows of the columns and palms in the dim provisional ballroom. She did not return to Lady Gordon's waning throng until she was sure her eyes were dry. When she did, she wished she had run all the way home.

"Here you are!" Lady Gordon cried. "You've been invited to sing. Say you will." The ladies and the gentlemen behind them watched Julia expectantly. She opened her mouth to refuse, but Captain Dewey stepped forward and took her hands.

"Of course she will. You sing like a lark, I am told."

Julia wondered what Greenway had told them. She had begged him not to volunteer her talent.

The group pleaded with her, and Lady Gordon guided her into another room where a pair of ladies performed cheerily on a pianoforte. They drifted away from their duet at Lady Gordon's commanding hint, and the room quietened. Julia thought she would faint. Remembering her courage on the island cay, she squeezed her eyes shut and pretended she was surrounded by smiling natives rather than expectant peers. The first few bars of her favorite song came to mind, and she found her voice. When she opened her eyes to measure the approval of the small audience, she noticed Mr. Greenway standing at the far door, his hands behind his back and his face unreadable. The sad lullaby made her eyes water.

CHAPTER EIGHT

Captain Dewey determined three days of leave would be fitting for his ship and crew, and although he spent most of his time at the quay squabbling with naval suppliers over canvas and spars, he found time to call on Lady Gordon and her ward every afternoon. He shared new details about his family, but nothing far beyond the fact he was a second son and had one younger brother who would take up the cloth.

Julia felt it appropriate to tell him about her father and mother, but she said little about Hiram and Caroline, as she suspected through Lady Gordon it was already well known her living relatives were not concerned with Julia or her future.

Lady Gordon insisted she sing again, and Julia did so with blushing modesty, hoping Captain Dewey did not think her too odd a bird. She did not share his enthusiasm for exchanging bloody battle stories between the Navy and the French, and it felt rather low to talk about other ladies on the island and their situations without them present. Lady Gordon however, did not feel it a crime to exchange information on who did what and with whom, and by the time Captain Dewey left every evening Julia's mind felt exhausted.

The captain took a turn with her on the grounds on each of his visits. They exchanged pleasantries and Julia's growing love of the Caribbean. He did not try to kiss her again, and she was glad. Perhaps he had realized his attention felt like pursuit, and she was not sure what she should feel or do.

On his final day before departing with orders in the *Triumph*, Lady Gordon invited him to dine. He happily accepted, and after he enjoyed his talk and cigars with the assemblyman in his study, he invited Julia out to the veranda to enjoy the night air. Lady Gordon smiled her permission, her eyes rounding with some unspoken encouragement in a long stare she aimed at Julia. Discomfited, Julia allowed the captain to take her arm, and they moved onto the veranda in the light of the waxing moon.

"It's much cooler here," she murmured, unable to resist the pleasurable feelings chilly ocean breezes had on perspiring ladies swathed in ridiculous amounts of layers.

"It's far better at sea," Dewey replied. "I never feel hot in the moonlight on deck."

"I'm sure you do not, but don't you miss the tops?"

Dewey laughed. "I confess, sometimes, I do, but I'm the captain, so if I want to scamper up the ratlines like a midshipman, I take it upon myself to do so."

"You aren't afraid of the heights?"

"No one can reef a sail and be afraid of flying over the waves."

Julia smiled. "I wish I was not so scared to be on top of the world."

"There's nothing to fear."

"Falling," Julia replied.

"That's just it," said Dewey in a thoughtful way, "you don't fall. No matter how high up you must climb, you put it out of your mind and hold on for life. Falling is not a possibility."

"What if it can't be helped?"

Dewey reached for her hand and squeezed it so tight she met his gaze. He stared deep into her eyes with such intensity she'd feel impolite to look away. "You're right, of course, as you usually are. Sometimes falling can't be helped."

Julia gave him a timid smile. As if it granted him some form of permission, he pulled her toward the stairs. "It's too dark," she said.

"Nonsense. We can see well enough to walk the grounds. It's easier to smell the night jasmine, and we can look out over the sea and make wishes."

"I'm not sure I can see the harbor in this moonlight. You have better eyes."

Dewey chuckled at her hesitation and led her across the veranda. They moved quietly down them with stealth, and Dewey took her arm as he led her quickly around the house into the sweet smelling night. "It's beautiful, isn't it?" He looked up at the sheet of stars overhead.

Julia dropped her head back on her shoulder. "Yes, I should say so."

"Come along, then." He led her across the acreage toward the last line of trees separating the grounds from the hillside that fell away to the turbulent, rocky river.

"Take care, Captain," Julia warned, when she saw he meant to lead her down the incline.

"I'm as sure footed as a goat," he teased.

She wasn't sure and pulled back, taking tiny steps and clinging to his elbow for support. They slipped just as the slope reached bottom, before it swept upward to the little knoll that overlooked the view. He caught himself and her, too, and she was grateful for his solid strength. "I'd tumble all the way down if there wasn't this small rise. It's a perfect vantage point to see all around the island."

"Well," said Dewey, pulling her up onto the grassy mound, "you won't be able to see very far this night, but that is not the purpose."

"What is the purpose?" The wind felt strong. It whipped loudly up the hillside. Julia thought if she listened hard enough she could hear the rambling river, too. She waited for Dewey's reply, but he looked lost, staring at her again.

"My purpose," he whispered, "is to take you into my arms at the highest point above the sea so we can fly."

Julia blushed in the darkness, and he swept her up in a warm embrace. "This isn't the highest point of the island," she corrected him, "that's Boggy Peak."

"Does it matter?" he said, his nose touching hers. Her feet were off the ground, and she could hardly breathe in his tight hold.

"I suppose not. No, not at the moment." He set her gently on her feet, and her arms fell naturally around his neck. She thought he might kiss her again and so slid her arms down his chest and took a small, backward step.

He startled her by dropping to one knee and reaching for her hands. He held them in a tight, steady grip, while the rushing air seemed to spin the world around her. "My purpose, Miss Scott, is to ask for your hand; to beg of you to make me the happiest of all men."

The distant stars became smudges of light as Julia's eyes blurred. Her heart had flip flopped when he'd taken a knee, but the proposal from his throaty voice made it slow to a dull, steady like march.

"Oh, Captain, I—"

"Say you will," he pleaded, but it was only his words that begged for her approval. His tone was all confidence and charm.

Julia swallowed. She wavered on trembling feet. Why did this feel like Mr. Carver all over again? Dewey was a captain of the Royal Navy, with a respectable family and a fine future. He was young, and a handsome man, far more striking than her in looks. An involuntary gasp made Julia realize she held her breath. She struggled for something to say to put him off so she could think.

"Say yes."

"Captain Dewey, I am flattered beyond words... You've made me feel welcome and happy and admired."

"Then it is as I intended."

"But—"

"Yes?"

Julia swallowed a knot in her throat the size of a melon. She coughed and put a hand to her chest." I'm not certain," she admitted. "It's so sudden. I must have time to think about it."

Dewey rose to his feet slowly, gripping her hands as if she were his safety line in a tempest. "You cannot call us sudden, love, we have been attached since I first pulled you from the sea." He reached out and stroked a loose lock of Julia's hair, fluttering about her face in the whipping wind.

His words brought Julia's galloping emotions to a halt. "But you did not believe me. You asked me to leave your ship."

Dewey pierced the swirling air with sharp, loud laughter. "That was your family's doing no doubt. They sent you away, defenseless, to the middle of the dangerous world." He took her by the chin and pulled her to him until their noses touched again. "I saved you, my dear, and you will save me." He stared intently into her eyes and even in the darkness she could see they were pooled with desire. "Be my wife," he insisted. "You can live out your days with security and proper company here in Antigua. Or at home," he added, "with my family." He waved his arm out toward the sea in presentation. "Anywhere in the world, wherever my career takes me. You can be by my side."

He smiled, satisfied with his speech, and tried to draw her nearer. Julia resisted. Her mind spun like a top, and she felt any moment she would be sick. She would lose her dinner and humiliate herself before the most handsome, eligible bachelor who had ever proposed to her. In the back of her mind she saw Caroline gasp. Captain Dewey was her second proposal and probably the last. She would be twenty and one before the year's end. Her chest squeezed tightly, and her stomach seized into knots. It felt as if she'd eaten glass shards for dinner. She pulled her hands away and bent over, holding her sides to keep from crying out. "I cannot," she said. The words hurt from the inside out to utter.

"What's this now?" Captain Dewey sounded stunned. After a long hesitation, he pulled her back to him to comfort her and ease the pain. "You must, Miss Scott," he whispered in her ear above the night winds. "I have proposed, you must accept, and we will be married; by the admiral himself if you wish it."

Tears pricked Julia's eyes, and one freed itself. It rolled silently down her cheek. The entire affair felt wrong. "I cannot accept you," she whispered back. "Not now. Not so soon."

Dewey reared back as if she'd struck him. "What can you mean? You've accepted all my attentions and spent more time with me than you have with anyone." His tone sounded on the edge of anger, and it frightened her.

She took another step back, but her heel was unable to find solid ground to support her. Stumbling, she caught herself on his coat. Before she could catch her breath and right herself, he brought her back to him and squeezed again. She felt like a juiced lemon. "Captain," she repeated, her eyes brimming, "I cannot marry you. I'm not ready, and I'm not sure. Please, let me go."

"I will not let you go," he said stubbornly. He buried his face in her neck, and she felt the hard pressure of his mouth on her skin.

"No, don't." Julia tried to wriggle free, but his hold on her was firm. For some reason, the image of Mr. Greenway came into her mind. She knew he would not approve of her doing such things with Captain Dewey. It was his opinion, she realized, that mattered most to her.

"You will marry me." The captain looked up, and his gaze frightened her. It was not the officer she knew, but a demanding, spoiled child. "You have no connections here besides your uncle, and no one else is as willing as me to take you on with no fortune or inheritance."

"Take me on?" Julia put her hands on his chest and pushed herself away. "Captain Dewey, I am in no need of anyone besides my dear uncle to take me on."

He laughed. "You! You're the niece of an admiral of the blue, Miss Scott. We are a perfect match. You are the woman for me, even without a large income or title."

His acknowledgement of what she lacked she found offensive. She shook her head with vehemence. "I am a lady," she insisted, "but I am not the lady for you. I'm sure of it. I like you immensely, but that is all."

"It's enough." His voice turned cold and sharp, like the icicles that hung from the eaves in the dead of Netley Hall's dark winters. It gave her the shivers.

"I said no." Julia no longer felt sorry or confused but all the more sure. His manners were questionable at least, his motives at most. What if Greenway had been right? All Captain Dewey could speak about was her uncle. That much was true.

The night sounds around them stilled as if listening to their disagreement. In the quiet, with a penetrating stare, Dewey said, "You will marry me, Miss Scott, and there will be no further discussion about it between us."

His declaration was so bold, she felt her eyes widen. For a moment she could think of nothing to say. Her hands fell to her sides, and her heart pounded with thick, heavy anxiety. She shook her head, miserable. It was home all over again. It was Papa dying, and Caroline ruling with iron gloves. It was Hiram's failure to save his only sister. It was the long voyage across the sea with nothing but fears to propel her forward to hope and a new life. She put a hand to her throat, and felt the rapid pace of her lifeblood. Forward, on to hope. That faint stroke of courage had pulled her through terrible times. Had she escaped her cage to be trapped by this officer once again?

"No, Captain," she said, in a voice cracking with trepidation. "I will not marry you, and that is my final word."

She was not sure that she meant it, but she knew she wanted to leave him to clear her mind. She turned sharply to go, but his arms shot out before she could escape. He pushed her hard, with flat hands and great force. Julia flew backwards into the air. She slammed down onto the steep hillside in a heavy heap below the knoll, then rolled head back over heels like a wild carriage wheel out of control, spinning and crashing for what seemed like leagues of black, churning nothingness.

JULIA GASPED FOR AIR in one choking breath. When the world stopped spinning, and she could feel pain in her head, neck, and shoulders, she opened her eyes to see if she was dead. She was lying face down on moist, sandy earth. Something tickled her ear, and she tried to move so she could scratch it. The burning sensation on her arms and legs became stronger. She moaned.

With all of the remaining energy she possessed, she rolled over with a groan. The sky overhead was heavy with clouds that blocked out stars here and there. The sound of rushing water came from nearby. The dark silhouettes of nearby trees and foliage took sharp, jagged shapes. She licked her lips and tasted blood.

How far she had tumbled she did not know, but one thing she was sure of, Captain Dewey had not tried to stop it.

She moved an arm that ached but did not hurt badly enough to be broken. Gingerly, she wiped her face with her sleeve and rested her arm across her forehead. Perhaps if she lay there long enough, someone would come along and find her in the tangled ravine and carry her back to the house. She wondered how long it would be before Lady Gordon would worry. Regardless of his actions, surely Captain Dewey had rushed back to the house for help. Someone would arrive soon.

A plop of water smacked her chin, and she moved her arm so she could see. Another drip hit her eye. She winced, squeezing her eyes shut and gingerly trying to sit up before it began to pour. Too late, the fast moving storm began to shower down, drenching the island with sharp raindrops that fell in slanted sheets. Julia managed to crawl up on to her knees, but bobbled before she could stand. The rain soaked through her clothes instantly. It ran through her hair in rivulets and down the sides of her face. Burning and hurting from head to toe, she forced herself to her feet with a gasp and limped blindly toward the shadows of what she hoped was tree cover and not another drop that might finish her off. The force of the rain shower receded as she dragged herself beneath the towering branches of a wide ancient tree. Exhausted, she rested her forehead on the cool, hard bark and tried to think while rain showered around her.

A faint sound behind her made her flinch and spin about in fear. She expected to see Captain Dewey intent on rescuing her, but a scream rose in her throat. When the tall, dark shadow came close enough into focus, she knew only that it wasn't Dewey, and she could not speak. It was too late.

The night spun around her and so did fear, but she forced herself to stay alert as she pushed the black stranger away. "No," she managed to utter as the strong force picked her up like a sack of flour and tossed her over his shoulder. The action punched the air out of her again and for several breaths she could not breathe.

AFTER FLOPPING ALONG like a rag doll in the pitch dark of night, Julia was eventually handed over to another pair of solid, strong arms. When she was set down, she knew promptly from the light swaying sensation and damp beneath her head that she had been laid in the bottom of a boat. She stared up at the steady stars still in place, unmoved by the rainstorm that had swept over the island like a broom. Any moment she expected to be beaten or worse.

The lapping of water over rocks and shore told her that she had been carried down to the beach. The wet, musky scent of wood and unperfumed bodies told her she was once again a prisoner of men. What kind of men she did not know, but they were not Englishmen. Forcing herself to find one crumb of courage within, she whispered loudly, "Captain?" The only reply was an increase in the sound of quiet murmurs in something other than English. Her mind raced at the familiar language. She knew that tongue. She heard it up and down the sandy roads and sometimes in the marketplace.

"Smith?" she uttered with one last gasp, but there was no response. It was the wrong name, she knew it, what she had meant to say was Greenway. She closed her eyes and tried to find a deep hole for her mind to fall into, but fear kept her tensed and ready. The boat launched, and the dark men around her began to paddle, the watercraft slipping smoothly away from the island on silent wings. She feared to sit up less someone push her back down. Her body throbbed with pain. Time passed in a void until she could no longer keep her eyes open. She did not know where she would awake, or what would be her fate. Sleep won.

PAIN CARRIED HER TO sleep, and pain woke her up again. She flinched when she came to. Her body was moved like a piece of furniture, from one boat into another. As she was passed over the side in the rosy light of dawn, she looked down at the dugout canoe below her and saw black men who looked like slaves in the dim light of the new day.

For a few snatches of thought, Julia felt a sense of déjà vu and a part of her expected to be tossed onto a smooth planked deck and find Captain Dewey standing at attention. She cried out, and someone whispered her name. Instead of being butchered or drowned, she was carefully handed over to someone with a familiar linen shirt and a strong but soft embrace. He smelled faintly of salt and jasmine. When his face came into focus, she found herself looking into the dark eyes of Mr. Greenway. Concern and fatigue etched his face, and she thought he looked as if he had missed a night's sleep. So relieved was she to find herself in his arms that she almost drifted back off into a welcome respite, but he brushed a coarse hand against her cheek.

"Julia?" he murmured, and she forced herself to look again. "Are you hurt?"

She sucked her bottom lip again and found it sore and chapped. "Greenway," she whispered, afraid to make any more effort less it pained her. She took a deep breath and made herself concentrate. "Savages... on the island. No. Slaves. On the river."

It was the best she could do to get her point across. Greenway did not seem to comprehend it, or he found her suggestion of runaway slaves attacking Antigua to be all in good sport.

"There are no savages here," he muttered. "Just friends." He set her down on a long narrow bench and covered her with a warm blanket. She sniffed again and smelled fish. It was so strong she wrinkled her nose. After a time, when she felt she could move her head, she found him beside her. "Where are we?" Her throat was dry and hoarse.

"Your favorite place," he teased, "in a boat at sea."

She looked about. The boat was no more than a half the length of a modest schooner from bow to stern. Only a few men labored about pulling lines while others tied them off. "We're not lost?"

"No," Greenway said, flashing his good teeth and humor together. "Just out a-fishing," he said in a singsong voice.

"How did you find me?"

She looked about the deck again for dark men, but there were none. "I thought—"

"I will make it as simple as possible for you to understand and ask for your forgiveness." His penitent expression made her look deep into his eyes, to see if he was teasing.

"What have you done?" Her chest tightened with worry.

"To be frank, I asked a few associates to keep an eye out for anything unnatural around the Gordon's property. Fortunately, some of them were on the way up river when they heard you tumble down the hill."

"Those dark men?" Julia wondered. "They are friends?"

"Yes, old and trustworthy friends."

"I thought at first it was those savages again with their king."

Greenway chuckled and leaned over as if his remarks were confidential. "He wasn't a king exactly, and you may set your mind at ease. He's over you now."

The silliness of his reply made Julia grin, despite her undignified circumstances. She wondered what slaves would be doing upriver in the dark of night and asked it out loud. Greenway replied shortly, "There are many kinds of business around Antigua. None we should speak of for now."

She didn't know what he meant but instead of asking more said, "Is this your fishing boat?" She watched a sailor cast a long net out across the smooth, morning waves.

"I own a share," he admitted. "As luck would have it, my acquaintances knew right where to bring you when they found you on the riverbank."

"Oh." Julia blinked. She examined the rest of the crew aboard Greenway's ship and noticed some of them were black men, too. "How convenient, I suppose."

"It might have been a look out," Greenway mumbled under his breath, but when she asked him to repeat it he pretended to be deaf.

"So this is what you do when you're away," she said trying to pull more out of him.

He shrugged. "It is best not to go into detail right now. You may find it difficult to understand."

Uncomfortable, Julia shifted in her seat, and Greenway slid closer so she could lean on him. His arm went around her tired shoulders. "Are you well? Do you need a physician?"

Julia shook her head. "I don't suppose I do. I'll recover from this tumble, too. I'm just bumped and bruised."

"And scraped," Greenway said with a frown. He stretched out her arm to its full extension and turned it so she could see the red and brown scratches from falling over the exposed twisted tree roots.

"It doesn't hurt so much anymore," she promised. He took her arm gently into his lap.

"I've sent word ahead to Sir Henry. I imagine his wife will be beside herself." Greenway shifted his glance from the rising buttermilk-colored sun to Julia's profile again. "Did I not warn you to stay away from the hilltop without me, even to draw? And to wander down there in the dark, too." She felt his eyes sweep over her from head to toe. "You're a mess, Miss Scott," he scolded, but his kind tone said he did not mean it. "Your new gown is torn and stained, and there's nothing left of your stockings. What happened to your pumps?"

"I do not know," Julia countered in a soft tone. She met Greenway's studious examination but hesitated to say more.

"What is it?" he asked.

"My hair feels like a bird's nest."

"So it is."

His truth didn't bother her one bit. To say she looked ravishing would be a lie. She considered telling him more; that she had not been alone, but she wasn't sure she wanted to see Greenway's reaction. What would he do if he knew the truth?

They enjoyed an agreeable length of silence before he edged away from her to find something to eat and drink. When she felt well enough to refresh herself, she was taken below to a low cabin and washed herself up although there was no choice but to remain in her clothes. She returned to the deck and the hands made a patch of shade for her to rest under by stringing up a sheet of canvas to block out the sun. When he wasn't speaking with the tanned old captain or the crew, Greenway joined her under the little canopy, and they talked about the admiral and what she should do when she joined him at last. Greenway was not concerned about the rainy season ahead, but he near frightened Julia to death with stories of wild tempests and blows that blew away sugar cane and cattle, and flood waters that surged up over the hills with no warning, taking everything in their path.

"You make me feel I should not settle for any home less than on top of Boggy Peak," Julia warned him.

They ate their supper under the canopy as the sun began to lose its fight to stay aloft in the clouds. Its blinding light had lit up the hot day for the fishermen, but now looked as golden and rich as precious metal.

"My home is safe enough," Greenway said unexpectedly. He fiddled about with strips of fish and pieces of breadfruit the captain had offered his guests. It was not a luscious meal, but it was better than nothing at all.

"I wouldn't know," Julia teased. "I haven't been invited to your address."

Greenway scrunched up his face. "I don't have many dinners or guests for that matter. Entertaining is not on my list of priorities."

"You are nothing but entertaining if you are anything at all," Julia disagreed.

"Oh, I'm a charming guest," relented Greenway with a laugh, "but that's part of my trade."

"What do you do?" Julia pressed. "Whether you are truly a merchant or agent or even accountant, I cannot tell."

"I suppose," Greenway said with some reluctance, "one would call me a corsair of sorts."

Julia turned this over in her mind. Her disquiet must have shown on her face.

"You find the occupation of privateering disreputable, do you?"

"I only mean that I have heard it's... well, Mr. Greenway, what *were* you doing on that pirate ship?"

He smiled again, but this time it was not impudent. "I own several ships, as well you know. I partner with several merchants and do business with certain trading companies. I am not a privateer, but I do see to the success of our ships making port."

"Yes?" Julia urged.

"Sometimes, I am asked to see personally to problems that afflict... business."

"I don't understand," Julia admitted. "You owned part of that pirate ship?"

Greenway grimaced. "I did not. To be frank, Miss Scott, and trusting in your confidence, I do have a history in the army but did not wish to keep my rank or purchase another. When there are issues that harm business in the Leewards, I sometimes take it upon myself for myself or certain... clients, to take care of the problems firsthand. Sometimes I board a ship as myself, other times... I just board."

"So you were only pretending on that ship?"

Greenway bobbed his head slightly. He set down his tin plate and wiped his hands on a worn towel that had been wrapped around two pieces of biscuit.

"I signed on with those men in Tortuga. It was my intention to learn their routes and discover their hideouts. Every ship's bottom must needs be cleaned eventually."

"Then I came along and got in your way."

"It was all in good timing," Greenway assured her. "I did not participate in their pillaging, and so after a time my secret would have been discovered."

Julia remembered the man who had shoved her against the bulkhead and what Greenway had done to him. "I never meant to put you in a position," she said sorrowfully, "to kill a man."

Greenway rested a hand on her knee. He watched her steadily. The setting sun made the sky look golden purple, and it reflected in his eyes. "I never hope for such things, but I thank God I have the training and experience to hold my own."

"I thank Him, too," Julia said with a soft smile. She couldn't look away from his honest, tender gaze. How different he was than Captain Dewey. How rugged and authentic was his nature, and his looks matched it.

"Those men on the river who brought me to you? They weren't slaves?"

After a long pause, Greenway glanced at her then around the near empty deck. "Slavery will be abolished in the colonies," he said in a quiet whisper. "There are a great many already seeing to its demise. As for myself, perhaps my ships have use for moving a great many things away to safer places—besides silks and ribbons."

"Oh," Julia responded.

"We mustn't speak of such things." Greenway put a finger to his lips.

Julia reached up and brushed a wisp of dark hair behind his ear. He had knotted it at the nape of his neck but work and wind had pulled it out. He looked blowsy and wild. He smiled and his green eyes crinkled around the corners. He could not be more than seven or eight years her senior, but he carried far more poise and wisdom. She moved her hand down his face until it reached his chin, and she gave it a small squeeze. "You are the most curious man I have ever met," she admitted.

"Well," he said with a mild smirk, "I'm not so beautiful as you or important as your uncle, but I'm smarter than your brother and kinder than your stepmother."

"You're twice as dashing as Captain Dewey."

He rounded his eyes, feigning shock. "Are you so sure?"

She giggled. "I'm sure."

"I'm not half so rich as some men in Southampton," he admitted, "nor London or Bath, but I have a home and clothes good enough for balls and dinner with an assemblyman."

Julia teasingly raked him over from his hopeless hair to his bare feet. "You're dressed like a poor fisherman today," she observed, "but I've seen you in much less and much worse." The memory of him in beads and loincloth made her erupt with laughter. He joined in, not the least bit chagrined that she laughed at him. Her thoughts moved from his improper attire to his bold attempts to have her spied on while he was away.

"So your friends were watching over me while I stayed at the Gordon's home. Was this in the event Captain Dewey acted in the least bit impetuous?"

He became serious again, although light glimmered in his eye as a happy twinkle. "I did, Miss Scott. I've taken to you like a cat to cream, and ask for your apologies that I did not trust the man. I see now, I cannot blame him. A brave girl with Caribbean eyes who wants to know her own mind is great temptation."

His words filled her heart with some strange elation. Julia swallowed and tried to smile. She swiped the hair off her forehead and pushed it down useless on her tangled crown. Greenway reached up and smoothed it for her. His probing gaze searched her eyes, and she found herself moving toward him pulled by some unseen force in her heart. She wanted, at the very least, to fill the aching, empty hole in her soul with his energy and touch. She moved to brush her cheek up against his firm jaw, but turned her head in surprise at the invitation in his eyes which had softened into muddy green pools. Her eyelids fluttered shut on their own accord when his warm lips touched hers. Her swirling, twirling spirit danced with the evening breeze and leapt with joy. She slid her arms around his neck, melting into a delicious warmth and security that felt like home.

CHAPTER NINE

They sailed against the evening tide as twilight pushed the sun beneath the footrest of the heavens with a determined lilac shove. It was early the next afternoon before the fishing vessel swayed on its moorings in the gentle curve of Falmouth Bay. It laid a stone's throw away from the naval yard over a narrow peninsula. Julia did her best to stay out of the way of rigging and crew from a small perch at the stern where she watched mobs of gulls dive for scraps left behind by fisherman. The birds shrieked and scolded one another over the salty wind and calls of seamen.

With her chin nestled into her bare palm, she wondered what Lady Gordon would say when Mr. Greenway once again escorted her up from the shore to her home. Julia's gown was tattered and her hair tangled and wild even in its pert, long braid not too different than the fishtails worn by the crew. She had not confided in Mr. Greenway exactly how she fell from the sandy knoll above the river, and did not know what to expect when she saw the captain again. Had he hurried to the house with some explanation? Would it do to make an accusation against him? She shivered involuntarily at the idea of confronting the man who had shoved her to a near death. Perhaps he had only meant to push her away and did not consider she might fall.

Julia grinned in spite of herself. They would not imagine that a dugout canoe of free Africans might rescue her from the river bank and paddle her out to sea to reunite with her West Indies hero.

She sighed, and a happy stream of affection coursed through her veins and made her heart pitter patter. Mr. Greenway was many things to her, she realized. He had been nothing but proper if he had harbored feelings before now. His declarations the day before hinted to her of something deep and sincere, an authentic affection and respect like no one had ever expressed toward her before. It was providence he should not only rescue her, but become her friend. To think that there could be more between them filled her with endless excitement. She hoped she did not make presumptions because he had kissed her, but it was not the same with Captain Dewey and his pomp and circumstance. It had felt real, honest, and pure. If a kiss could last forever, she would want it to be her kiss with him.

She smiled to herself and blinked against the shifting rays of the penetrating sun. With no bonnet, she was forced to make do with Mr. Greenway's worn tricot, which smelled as leathery and sun worn as ever, but it was a scent that suited the hat as well as the crown it covered.

Greenway drew her away from her reflections with a squeeze on her shoulder. "Are you ready?" She looked up into his bright eyes and felt satisfied that he looked happy to be with her even if she would be deposited once more with his cousins until her uncle returned.

"I am, I suppose. Though what I shall tell Lady Gordon, I have no idea."

"The truth will do," he said easily, as all things of good common sense came easily to him.

She took his proffered hand, and he helped her disembark after the kindest of compliments to the captain. "You won't have to walk this time," Greenway announced as they reached the level landing of the street bordering the quay. He motioned toward a modest carriage hitched to two handsome horses, and a driver who looked expectantly back at them.

"Has Sir Henry sent us horses?"

"No," Greenway replied. "This is my carriage. I did not send word or explanations to the Gordon's until a half hour ago. There's no point in making a scene, although from what I have already heard, soldiers from the battery are searching the river for you, and some of the fisherman are watching for your body in the shallows."

Julia shuddered. "That's a bit grotesque, but I don't suppose they had any other way of knowing.

"They'll know the truth soon enough," Greenway promised. "We have much to tell them." He seemed to imply more than Julia's tumble down the hill, and her stomach fluttered at the idea he might publicly express his attachment to her. As they climbed into the carriage, it was as if he could read her thoughts. He took her hand and held it tight, occasionally rubbing his thumb over her fingers absent-mindedly. He did not seem to mind she had received too much exposure to wind, sun, and sea without her gloves and a proper bonnet.

Julia recognized he only followed the rules of propriety when necessary. When they were alone, she did not have to worry about her looks, her words, her dress, or even her situation. It made her feel even more attached to him, and she squeezed his hand back and smiled when she caught him studying her.

"I'm sure I look as frightful as I did the first time you brought me to the island. I'm going to run out of convincing excuses and gowns to be sure."

"Your uncle has allotted a generous account for your needs and wants. And you need not be concerned, he has paid me back for your wardrobe when we first arrived."

"I owe you both the world," Julia said with earnestness. "The sun and the moon and the stars if I could hold them in my hands."

Mr. Greenway smiled at her, and she loved the creases around his eyes. The carriage jerked along, winding its way up the steep incline toward the island's hilly plateau where plantations spread out in no pattern or sense, and the sugarcane grew up high and green.

When the Gordon's home came into view, Julia caught her breath. She realized the time to face Captain Dewey would be soon. She pressed her fingers nervously into Mr. Greenway's palm, wishing he could know of her anxiety. She'd seen what he would do to anyone who tried to harm her, but Dewey was no pirate and a duel would be scandalous. She sighed at the idea of two men making a fuss of someone so insignificant as she. The other women on the island, especially the older, unmarried ones who watched Mr. Greenway with funny, fawning expressions would push her out of their circles immediately.

"You seem nervous," Greenway observed. Julia tilted her head back noting his cheeks had received a good deal more of sun since she'd taken his hat.

"I'm glad you are with me again, to be sure."

"It is not a problem, not for me or for them. Anyone could take a tumble from the knoll, although you must admit you will have to offer some explanation as to why you were out wandering the grounds alone at night. Were you sketching?"

The carriage pulled into the drive and crunched over the pea size gravel toward the great gray house with its cheerful flower strewn veranda. "Mr. Greenway," Julia said. She looked down at their entwined fingers and decided to be truthful. "I was not alone on the knoll. Captain Dewey had asked me to take a turn after dinner."

"You were on the knoll with the Captain?"

"Yes." She nodded and held on to his hand. "I did not want to go. I did not think it proper, but Lady Gordon did not seem to mind us on the veranda, and he talked me into a stroll around the grounds."

"What were you doing on the knoll when you slipped and fell?" Greenway's voice dripped with curiosity, and a bit of his habitual sarcasm could be heard.

Before he could become angry, Julia blurted out, "He asked me to marry him, and I didn't want to. He wouldn't accept such an answer, and when I insisted I could not, he... pushed me." Julia stopped abruptly. Near winded from her explanation, she took a heavy breath and then with some degree of trepidation looked to see if Greenway would believe her or not.

His face went through a chain of expressions that made her brace herself for one of his stone cold and fierce denunciations. He looked at her as if to question her more, but looked away. The carriage pulled up to the house, and they both noticed the flurry of activity through the louvered windows.

"I guess they are expecting me," Julia said wistfully. She turned to Greenway and pled, "Don't be angry with me, please. I didn't know what would be proper to do or say, and I'm..." another rush of truth rushed out of her, "I'm afraid of Captain Dewey. I don't think he's quite right."

Rather than look angry or disappointed, Greenway gave a short, barking laugh. He jumped down in one easy leap then raised his arms up for Julia to fall into. With relief, she leaned into them, and he swept her out of the carriage before the driver could assist them either one.

Greenway took her by the chin, lifted his hat off her head, and placed it back on his own, then he whispered, "*You* are quite right and have no reason to ever think otherwise." His faith in her felt like a kiss. He placed her hand on the crook of his arm and walked her up the stairs into the house without ringing the bell. After being welcomed by a flummoxed Roberts, he pushed open the doors to the drawing room to greet Lady Gordon and her company.

Stepping into the familiar room felt like coming home. Lady Gordon jumped to her feet and clapped her hands together in joy. She picked up her skirts like she might dash across the room and snatch Julia up in a jubilant embrace, but the woman who remained sitting across from the lady's settee, froze everyone in the room with her shrill, grating voice.

"Upon my word, Julia Scott. You look like a filthy puppy someone's dragged through the mud."

Julia's lips formed the words, but it took great effort to stutter out a greeting. "Caroline." She tried to curtsey, but her knees cracked, and she froze. Clinging to Mr. Greenway's arm she thought he might have to pull her back to her feet.

GREENWAY FOUND HIS tongue first. He bowed and glanced at Lady Gordon who looked with excitement at Caroline and said, "May I introduce you to Mr. Greenway, a well respected gentleman on the island and my husband's cousin, and of course, your lovely step daughter you do already know."

Greenway acknowledged Caroline with a cool dip of his chin. Caroline narrowed her eyes. Julia knew it as an appraisal of his income, class, and title.

"Mr. Greenway," Lady Gordon finished, "Mrs. Scott of Netley Hall."

"Mrs. Scott," he finally acknowledged, when she did not offer a word to the pair of them.

Lady Gordon chuckled with nervousness. "You must be so happy to see your stepmother, Julia," she said, a faint streak of doubt clouding her face otherwise. She knew a bit of Julia's reasons for coming to the Indies, but whatever consternation she felt about Julia's family seemed to have been erased by Caroline's presence and whatever story she had told her.

"Of course she is happy to see me." Caroline's face magically brightened with a wide smile. "I am almost all the family she has as it is." She waved her hand like she and Julia were dear friends.

In a faltering voice, Julia asked the first question that came into her shocked mind. "Hiram... he has come?"

"Your brother? Of course not. He could not leave the estate. It won't run itself, my darling girl." She looked at Lady Gordon and laughed like Julia was an idiot.

Greenway squeezed her arm then guided her over to the settee and sat her down beside Lady Gordon. "She is a bit ragged, I fear, and needs rest and proper attire, but she came to no harm taking a tumble over the knoll above the river."

Lady Gordon put a hand on her heart, but Julia could not comfort her for Caroline's eyes were burrowing into her, telling her something to say or not to say, and she did not know which. She swallowed.

"Captain Dewey told us, of course." Lady Gordon inclined her head toward Mr. Greenway. "He came running the moment she fell, both horrified and full of joy that she had agreed to marry him, then fallen over the side in her excitement."

"Her what?" Greenway's eyes widened. He glanced at Julia, and she shifted her head, wanting to shake it vehemently but not wanting to make a scene. "That's not as I understand it," he said, pretending for Julia's benefit to be confused. "Why, someone fishing on the banks that night saw her tumble down and took her home until she could recover well enough to explain herself."

Caroline continued to stare. Julia tried not to be drawn in by her calculating gaze. She looked everywhere around the room instead. Lady Gordon put a hand to her knee. "Are you hurt?"

Julia forced a smile. "I am not. I was taken by boat around the island but handed over to Mr. Greenway as soon as I offered up his name."

"What a hero, your fisherman," she said. "I'm sure your mother and Captain Dewey will want to express their gratitude to him in person."

Julia took a deep breath and said firmly, "Mr. Greenway is my hero."

"Astounding," Caroline interjected. They all looked to see why she now rewarded them with conversation. "That you should rescue my stepdaughter and save her from certain death not once but twice."

Greenway smiled, but it was cutting. "What are the chances?"

Julia found herself twisting her fingers. Lady Gordon patted her again. "You should get changed, and lie down if you need to rest."

"I've rested well enough thanks to Mr. Greenway," Julia said with as much courage as she could muster. She was too afraid to leave Caroline in the room with people she loved and trusted, especially if Captain Dewey had spoken for her. She noticed her legs trembling and forced them to be still.

Greenway remained beside the settee, standing at her shoulder. It felt like reinforcement and gave her courage. She took a deep breath and let it out slowly, while the two women observed her.

"Well," Lady Gordon said in the uncomfortable silence, "let me be the first to congratulate you on your engagement, Julia."

Caroline smiled suddenly, and Julia thought she looked much like a cat with a cornered mouse. Greenway cleared his throat, and Julia opened her mouth forcing herself to speak. "There must be a misunderstanding." She turned her pleading eyes on Lady Gordon, knowing she would understand. "I'm sure there is no agreement."

Lady Gordon's happy look faded.

Julia forged ahead, pretending Caroline wasn't there. She'd rid herself of her once, and she'd rid herself of her once more. "We did have a conversation, I confess, but there is no understanding between us." She leaned back just enough so that her shoulder rested against Greenway's thigh.

"You must have hit your head," Caroline said. Her red hair was pinned up prettily on her head, but looked much like a twisting copper snake. Her bright eyes snapped with the perverse contradiction to Julia's words.

"I'm sure she is entirely of sound mind," interrupted Greenway.

"Oh no," she waved him away like a pesky gnat. "I've had the pleasure of meeting Captain Dewey, and he was very articulate." She smiled at Julia, feline-like again. "He is so fond of your uncle you know, and with his career and family living, more than worthy enough in my opinion to be so bold."

Julia felt her face redden from her distress. "We have no understanding," she repeated.

"Of course you do," Caroline corrected her.

Lady Gordon and Mr. Greenway fell silent, whether amazed at the conversation or confused, Julia wasn't sure. In a low, commanding tone, Greenway replied, "If the lady does not wish to marry, she won't be forced."

Lady Gordon turned somewhat pale, the color of linen. Her hands fluttered about until they found her handkerchief. Julia had never seen her put out.

"On the contrary, Mr. Greenway," Caroline said with astounding poise. "I am her mother after all, and if I approve of Captain Dewey's proposal then I must allow it. After all, her uncle will be delighted. Not that we don't appreciate your... interventions." She tossed her head a bit, looking very young and added, "Julia does not know her own mind well enough, and I'm sure a tumble down a dangerous bluff has entirely confused her."

Julia's heart shifted from its sickened thudding to a nervous pulse. Caroline had failed to force her to marry Mr. Carver and for whatever reason she approved of Captain Dewey, it appeared she would be as unyielding as stone when it came to the officer. Her stomach rolled over, and she thought she would be sick. It took too much effort to keep her knees from shaking, and she let them quake, sinking back further into the settee and against Greenway, her anchor. He said nothing. He had no authority here.

Lady Gordon cleared her throat and moved to stand, but to Julia's surprise, Greenway held out a hand to stop her. He eyed Caroline steadily like he wanted to do her great harm. Julia's heart began to hammer, and the sound of it echoed in her ears. She wanted to be brave and jump to her feet and rebel again, but the memory of Caroline smacking her to the ground cowed her. She would not be humiliated in front of Greenway. He thought too highly of her. She could not let him down.

"One moment, Lady Gordon," Greenway said in a stern tone. "Perhaps Mrs. Scott would like to know how her beloved daughter came to fall over the side of a dangerous bluff."

After only a small hesitation, Caroline said, "She's clumsy."

Beside her, Julia heard Lady Gordon gasp. "I'm sure she is not," she said, her voice raised with growing courage.

"Oh, but you don't know her. No matter. She will no longer be a burden to you here. I have ordered a carriage for tomorrow, and we will be carried away to my brother-in-law's residence across the island." She stared at Greenway. "Far across the other side of the island."

Julia's heart sank. She could bear it no more. Greenway had no idea with whom he dealt. There was no escape from Caroline. The only way out was to run away where she couldn't reach her with condemnations and make all of her decisions for her. Julia rose to her feet so quickly the room spun a bit, but she aimed for the door anxious to escape to her room and think of what to do. She must release poor Mr. Greenway from this unpleasant confrontation. She could ask no more of him.

Within two running steps she nearly managed her flight, but the drawing room door slammed open on its own accord, causing her to jump back in fright. Adorned in his naval blues and wholesome white breeches, Captain Dewey strode in with a look of avid determination. Julia could not believe her eyes. Their gazes met, and his piercing eyes warned her he would spin a tale as worthy as one of Caroline's exaggerations.

"Julia, my love," he uttered in a grief stricken voice. He held out his arms, and she shrank back. She would have thrown up her hands to push him away, no matter the scandal of the scene, but before she could react, Greenway's balled fist flew past her hot cheek. It connected with Captain Dewey's mouth, boxing him so hard and square, the officer sailed backward through the air and landed flat on his back with a horrific crash.

"Oh, my." Lady Gordon was the only one who could speak.

JULIA COULD NOT TURN her eyes away from the blood spurting from Captain Dewey's mouth. His lips and teeth were smeared with the stuff, and it dripped down his chin like red wine. "Oh, dear," Lady Gordon said again.

Greenway turned on his heel, remembering her presence. "You must excuse me, my lady," he said. He did not seem to find it queer to bow to her at this time, but he did swiftly and motioned toward the door. "Please, excuse us, won't you?"

Still staring at the bloodied man on the floor, Julia heard the rustle of muslin behind her. "Not you," Greenway said in a cold voice. She looked up to see he'd commanded Caroline to keep her seat. Lady Gordon hurried out, looking white and unsure of what she should do. Julia nearly sighed with relief when she remembered they were cousins by marriage, and surely she would not call on officers to make an arrest.

Julia twisted the sides of her thrashed gown anxiously. Captain Dewey did not appear in any hurry to stand. She was afraid of what would happen to him should he think it a good idea. Greenway solved her concern. He bent down and scooped Dewey up by the shoulders and shoved him hard against the drawing room wall.

The officer's eyes rounded with fear then drooped when he realized he would not be pummeled again. He spit a nasty red clot onto Lady Gordon's polished floor, and Julia gasped in disgust. He glanced at her then back at Greenway. "I didn't know you had intentions," he said through swelling lips. He gave a half laugh. "If you want the worthless wretch you may have her. She did agree to be mine, however." His gaze flitted back to Julia, and she answered, "I did not!"

"She's practically ruined," the captain sneered. Caroline made a noise behind her.

"He's lying." Julia's face burned with anger at his lies. "He did kiss me, but I'm not ruined."

Caroline sniffed and mumbled something under her breath. Distracted, Greenway turned like he wanted to question her, and Dewey took the opportunity to shove him away. He took a wild swing that barely grazed the tip of Greenway's nose. "You're practically a pirate," Dewey shouted. "A greedy, plundering trader making money on every island in the Leewards! Only your cousin's position allows you any suitability."

Dewey's weak accusation was another lack of good judgment. Julia jumped at the sound of Greenway's fist making contact again and the officer's wounded "oomph."

"Well," spat Caroline, and Julia spun about to find her stepmother at her heels. She stood eye to eye with her and determined this would be the last time she would ever be put in a position to defend herself from the woman's abhorrent machinations. A body hit the floor with a thud, and she figured it to be Dewey. Gathering courage, Julia thought of her father and mother who loved her and this woman who had every opportunity to do so, but did not.

"You," she said in a determined, low tone. Caroline did not flinch. "You have no business here in Antigua. I'm of age and owe you nothing."

Her stepmother smiled, but it was false and hateful. "You are an ugly duckling, Julia Scott, with strange eyes, no charm, and a dreadful complexion. You'll end up a starving spinster or woman of disgrace if I don't take control of you."

"Is that what her brother said to you?" Greenway's voice startled both Julia and Caroline, who had forgotten he was there.

"I imagine," said Greenway, "as I have known others in your position, that you left not long after Miss Scott. I suppose her brother was not happy to learn you had sent her away."

Caroline's eyes gave up nothing. She bit the inside of her lip though, and it made a small dent in her perfect features. Greenway stepped up behind Julia. She could feel the warmth from his exertions penetrating her clammy skin.

"You said Hiram agreed to it," Julia accused her. She forced herself to remain calm. With Greenway beside her she would get the answers she needed and with luck, some resolution.

"He agreed you should marry Carver," Caroline sneered. She focused in on Greenway. "She was engaged, you know."

"Yes," Greenway said with bored confidence. "I know all about it, and you."

Caroline's eyes darted back to Julia.

"I don't believe he knew about Carver after all," Julia guessed. "He did not know, and he did not tell you to send me away."

Caroline shrugged. Her delicate shoulders were sharp. "It does not matter what he wanted, you see. He spent all of our money, even your inheritance."

"He wouldn't have shipped me off." Julia needed to hear that it was true, and that her only living brother loved her and cared about what happened to her.

"You would have been a pauper." Caroline held up her hands as if the answer was obvious. "Mr. Carver was a simple solution."

"The poor man hardly knew how to speak to me," Julia said. "He was kind, but old and half-witted." Her voice raised a pitch, and she caught herself just in time from shouting.

"What does it matter?" Caroline smiled, trying to look genuine and like a motherly friend. "You made your way here, and you have connections thanks to your uncle."

"Ah," said Greenway, "I see it all now." He sighed heavily, disgusted with his conclusions. "You decided to travel abroad after you were tossed out, too. I would guess you meant to set your sights on the admiral."

Caroline blinked, and her face colored on the apples of her cheeks. Julia realized he had guessed it. "You came to pursue my uncle?" she said in horror, "to take advantage of his kindness toward me and... seduce him?" She curled her lips in disgust at the idea.

"Maybe a certain Captain should your uncle not find her inviting," Greenway added.

"Don't be ridiculous," Caroline jeered.

Julia's stomach rolled over on itself. "You make me ill. You used Papa, I can only guess it now. You cared nothing about me or Hiram or Netley Hall, only to find someone else to give you security."

"Security, perhaps," said Greenway, "but I suspect money is what she has in mind, or even a title if it comes with a living." He put his hands on Julia's shoulders and gently pushed her aside. "I believe," he said, directing his words to Julia but keeping his gaze on her stepmother, "that your brother has not spent all the money after all. If I were to wager for it, I'd bet Mrs. Scott is the guilty party, and only wishes she could find a way to take your dowry, too."

"You know nothing about me," Caroline hissed. She looked like she wanted to take a bite out of Greenway or claw out his eyes with her long, polished nails.

Julia's gaze dropped to the extravagant gold and pearl necklace woven around Caroline's neck. She shot an accusing glare at the woman who should have loved and cared for her. "It's true, then," Julia said in a weak voice. She felt like drifting down into a heap on the floor like a feather. "You are more terrible than I ever thought."

Distracted from Greenway, Caroline clucked her tongue at her. "If you would just marry the men I arrange for you, we could both be happy and terrible together." Her words sounded curt and biting.

Greenway cut her off from saying more. He moved in front of Julia like a shield. "The only man she is going to marry is me, you vile serpent. Now leave these grounds at once, before I expose your true integrity to the entire world."

Julia could not see her stepmother's face, but Greenway's words of 'marriage' and 'serpent' and 'leave,' while worlds apart, were joyful music to her ears. A wild adventurous mad, mad song.

Caroline's hesitation was long enough for Julia to sweep a glance beyond her shoulder to make sure Captain Dewey still lay groaning on the floor. She jerked when her stepmother strode around Greenway without warning. Caroline's arm flailed out to give Julia a slap, but Greenway struck it away and pushed her roughly toward the drawing room doors. "Get out," he snarled, and Caroline nearly tripped over Dewey's prostrate form rushing to escape. If Julia did not already know him, his abuse would have frightened her half to death. Her stepmother slammed the door behind them, leaving the room in silence.

Julia nearly collapsed before finding her way to the side chair and falling into it. She rubbed her temples, almost afraid of what Greenway would do next. She peered up when he crouched beside her on one knee. "You just rid me of the worst person to ever come into my life."

"She'll sail away no doubt," Greenway said. He took Julia by the hand. "I'm not too sure she won't land in St. Kitts or nearby, close enough to keep notice of you."

Julia frowned. "Don't fret," he whispered.

He pivoted toward Dewey, who had managed to rise to a seated position and rub his bloodied face. "Get out," he shouted, and the officer jumped. He scrambled to his feet like a drunk and shot them both a look of hatred before stumbling to the exit.

"Don't even think of a duel," Greenway called after him. "I can shoot a pea off a pinhead with one hand behind my back."

His audacious claim made Julia giggle. She put a hand over her mouth in regret when Greenway looked back at her with wide eyes. "You don't believe me?"

"Actually, I do," she admitted. "I was just trying to picture it."

"Well, imagine me in my very best." He looked down at his simple attire. His hair was loose from its knot, and rebellious strands splayed out around his ears. Julia smoothed them down. "You must wax your hair," she said sternly, "less grow it a little longer."

Greenway looked pointedly at her ruined gown. "Are you giving me fashion counsel?"

She laughed again, examining her deplorable state. "No, I should not. Should I?"

"You may," he said trying to wipe a smile from his face and be serious. "You may counsel me all you wish.

"May I?"

He nodded. His eyes beamed, a happy emerald green not unlike the canopy of the tropical trees on the island.

Julia put her hand to his cheek. "I am the one who appreciates your advisement, Mr. Greenway," she said softly. "I cherish your loyalty and your friendship and—"

"Friendship?" Greenway jerked his head back with a frown, as if the word was distasteful. "Is that all?"

Julia blushed and tried to keep from smiling. His grin grew serious at last. "I'm afraid I made a declaration, Miss Scott."

"What is that?"

Julia's hands had fallen to her lap, and Mr. Greenway took both of them up and raised them to his lips. "I told your stepmother I would marry you, and now I should keep my word."

Julia watched him scrutinize her and recognized the hope in his eyes. Her entire self swelled with a burning happiness she had never known, and she clasped his hands and raised them to her heart. "You should, Mr. Greenway. You should indeed!"

He held her cheeks with both hands and pulled her face to his. "What will poor Chief Pierre say? He'll have to find another turquoise-eyed sea sprite."

Julia tossed her head and laughed with happiness. "I don't care, *John Smith*, I don't care at all."

EPILOGUE

Admiral Hammond arrived in English Harbor overjoyed to reunite with his favorite niece and adamant, after she pled for mercy, that he should only demote the shameful Captain Dewey to a small gunboat. Her uncle next moved Julia across the island to his comfortable residence outside of St. John's, where he happily agreed to a banns for her and the reliable, if not mysterious, Mr. George Henry Greenway. Her account of the family's conduct since her father's death left the gentleman no choice but to write a stern letter of correction to her brother, and as to what he conspired with Mr. Greenway to do about her stepmother, she did not know. Mr. Greenway only promised her that she would never have to see or hear from the lady again. In her heart, Julia wickedly hoped the Carib chief had discovered her on his cay.

Mr. Greenway made another promise one week before the wedding when Julia found herself between the steep incline and sandy knoll below the Gordon's home. She'd promised to sketch the scene for her hero, and like Lady Gordon she meant to keep all of her promises.

Nearby, Greenway lolled about on an unsteady stool under the shade of an overgrown bush. He held a spyglass to his eye, examining the ships of which he controlled shares, and loudly complained about their lack of urgency.

"You are not in too much of a hurry yourself when you are at sea," Julia chided him. She examined the distant horizon with appreciation, and measured the ratio on her drawing.

"I hurry as much as I am able," he grumbled. He lowered the glass. "You did not find me idling when you were first snatched up by the unscrupulous lot who ran down your post-ship."

Julia turned to make a face at him. Beneath her bonnet, she wrinkled her nose. "I would hope you would never loiter if I find myself in such company again."

He jumped up and crossed the distance between them as fast as his legs would move. She almost flinched but remembered her downward tumble through the wild and steep vegetation.

"Now don't you fall again," he teased. He swept her up into his arms and spun her about, careful to keep them both on solid ground. "I cannot risk another rescue for such a clumsy girl. Your uncle will send you home straightaway."

"I'm not half so clumsy as I am accidental."

"What's that? It's one and the same."

Julia shook her head. "It's not." He set her down, and she reached down to pick up her drawing pages that fluttered in the breeze. "I cannot help it if I find myself in a bind because everyone around me wants to set my path."

With his arms still firm around her, Greenway said, "I promise I have no intentions of telling you how to set your sails." Julia smiled. He put his nose to hers and brushed it lightly. "Unless you set off in the wrong direction."

"So far my course has been straight and true. It led me straight to you." Julia swept her cheek over his then kissed him lightly on the nose.

He frowned, unsatisfied with her placement. "You seem to know where you are to go and what you are to do, but I must say you should pack better for your exploits."

"If you imply I have no idea how to attire myself for the West Indies, I'm sure you will often be quite right."

"You do have a wedding gown, I hope? Should I reach out to my contacts and find you something suitable?"

Julia grinned. "I'm sure it would not do to marry in beads and paint, much less a shift and bare feet."

"Then I will assume you will be properly attired when we make you Mrs. Greenway."

"With thanks to Lady Gordon you can be certain I will not shame your illustrious reputation."

"You have never brought me shame," Mr. Greenway whispered. "Not even with badly sketched rabbits or ridiculous feathers in your hair."

Julia bit her lip as his eyes trailed down to her mouth. "Then I will wear a head full of feathers on our wedding day, and give you all of my island drawings as your present."

"I have your trust and loyalty already. You sing for me whenever I wish. There's only one gift I yet hope for, Julia Scott, and that's you by my side every day."

Julia's eyes watered at the passionate emotions he stirred within her heart. She closed her eyes and let him kiss her, thinking wildly of her future joy in the arms of a West Indies gentleman and the shores of the Caribbean Sea.

~End~

BONUS MATERIAL

A Pirate at Pembroke

CHAPTER ONE

*S*ophie Crestwood felt nothing could be worse* than having a father who gossiped like a goose and a mother who read Gothic novels. Although it could be amusing at times, in truth she was long past her first Season and the only Crestwood at Leatherbury weathering serious reservations about her ability to find a husband.

Life at Leatherbury trotted along rather slowly compared to Town, but she liked it that way despite worrying about her lack of opportunity in the rolling hills of Higfield. Then there was Jack. He stood behind her, soaked and dripping water onto a lilac rug that protected the floorboards of her room.

She turned from her looking glass and pointed at the puddles. "Where have you been?"

"Swimming," he said without sorrow. He swiped at the copper cowlick that hung perpetually over his right eye to radiate more innocence.

Sophie was not ashamed of her youngest sibling, merely exhausted by him. In the farthest recess of her heart, he amused her, although he knew everything there was that tried her patience. Things she fancied disappeared. Things she did not fancy found their way under her bed or into the ivory armoire beside her dressing table. At her elbow rested a soft folded, cloth.

She handed it to him with a flick of her wrist. "What will Papa say when he learns you've skipped your Latin again?"

Jack dried off the best a twelve-year-old boy cared to do and handed her back the damp cloth. "Mr. Lyman doesn't care if I do my studies or not. He's overcome with his new volume of poetry and Margaret."

"Margaret?" Sophie's mind imagined housemaids with round cheeks and hips, and she flushed with understanding.

"Guess what I discovered?" Jack dared.

"The pond."

"No," he said, ignoring her wit. "I went over the rock wall to Pembroke and walked up to the house."

"Pembroke? Jack, you could have been shot. Someone lives there now."

"Do I look like a hare? Besides, no one was in the woods anyway." Jack cocked his head toward the door to hear if any of the servants were eavesdropping. "It's all commotion at Pembroke Hall, don't you know."

Sophie put a hand on her hip. "You ginger-haired devil."

"It's true. Mad Murdock's heir has come home. I seen the carts and wagons myself. There were heaps of strange looking things like we saw at the Bazaar."

Sophie maintained her look of severity, more at his grammar than his spying, but a morbid curiosity caused her to utter, "And?"

"Oh, I didn't see *him* as such, but the servants were there." Jack grinned with such wickedness his brown sun spots glowed. "They wore monkey jackets and tar caps and had pigtails down to their backsides."

"That doesn't make them pirates." Sophie gave a little shake of her head. "They are men who've come home to rest until the press gangs hunt them down again." A short ride from Portsmouth, Higfield was no stranger to the Navy press.

"They looked like pirates," Jack insisted in a loud whisper. His moss-colored eyes shined. "They was so fresh I could smell the salt and tar."

"You're ridiculous."

"I know what I seen."

"What you *saw*," Sophie corrected. Jack exercised a terrible grammatical habit, not to mention vocabulary when he became irritated or excited. It gave him the air of a lowly Jack Tar, an idea he relished.

"They're brown and withered like bad fruit, and one had a fishhook hanging from his ear. It's a whole band of buccaneers from the Indies. They've come to hide out at Pembroke Hall."

Sophie's breath escaped in a laugh. "You, dear brother, have been listening to rumors. Why would they come to England? The gibbets are here. The poor man living there now just happens to be a captain who's inherited, and it's about time, too. Why, I've watched Pembroke crumble to the ground my entire life. I imagine it was grand once upon a time, but—"

"Papa says—"

"Papa?" Sophie chided him, for everyone knew Mr. Crestwood's penchant for embellishment. "Go change your clothes before you catch a chill." Sophie pointed to the door.

"Pretty Sophie," Jack muttered, "you don't know nothin' at all."

"I know you shall be late for supper, and Papa will complain about it until the very last candle goes out." She shut the door behind him and finished pinning up her hair without any help. Where was Margaret when she actually needed her? "Pretty Sophie," she sniffed.

Despite her grimace, Jack's compliment pleased her. She was neither gifted with a great mind like their elder brother, Richard, nor as fearless and brave as Jack. Her music and netting were very well indeed, but any young lady could claim those accomplishments.

A bell rang for supper. Ignoring it, she frowned. Very little, Sophie worried, laid beneath the fair complexion and deep-set eyes that mirrored her movements in the looking glass as she smoothed down the pleats of her gown. "Pretty as a doe," was how Jack described them when feeling complimentary. "Dull as church," he amended when being a dog.

Sometimes Leatherbury and its occupants rubbed up against one another's nerves like harsh wool. Besides Jack's efforts, this occurred most often at the supper table while Papa mused over the latest tittle-tattle, and it began quite early this late afternoon.

"Carrots," Mr. Crestwood said with pleasure. "We haven't had a crop like this in so many years." He closed his eyes like they melted over his tongue.

"They are very good, Papa," Jack agreed, although they were from the cellar, last year's, and quite chewy.

This only encouraged Papa, who informed them his last dinner at Lady Mary's estate was no comparison when it came to the carrots at Leatherbury. Their carrots had not been half so capital, if he did say so himself, and didn't Mrs. Crestwood agree?

"Of course, you're right," murmured his wife, "I do not prefer the carrots at Oak Grove."

Sophie raised a brow and glanced at her mother because this was a perfect opening for a little teasing, but Mama had a faraway look which meant her thoughts were back in the library with her most recent novel.

"I don't remember the carrots at Oak Grove," said Sophie in a loud voice. She studied Jack and saw his mind scrambling for more conversation. He was waiting for an opportunity to speak, so he could draw away attention from the fact he'd neglected his studies, much like he had done at boarding school. She knew her brother would argue the pursuit of a naval career necessitated the skills of wading and floating more than schooling.

"How were your lessons this afternoon, Jack?" She smiled as she took another bite of carrots and decided they tasted very good indeed.

"I don't recall," Jack replied. "Papa, any news from Pembroke?"

"Ah," said their father, raising his fork in the air, "Sir Edward's heir arrived just yesterday from the Indies. They say it took four carts to bring his belongings up from Portsmouth, and there are more on the way. Can you believe it? How many things can a man possibly keep aboard a boat?"

"A ship. He's a captain, Papa," Jack reminded him. "He can use the entire hold to stow his valuables if it pleases him."

"A captain, that's right." Mrs. Crestwood's comment surprised them all. She cleared her throat, took a drink, and set the goblet back on the oblong table with a light hand. "No doubt Mr. Murdock has led an exotic life."

"*Captain* Murdock," Jack said under his breath.

Papa nodded. "Yes, and to be an heir, too. It makes no sense at all. How he came into his epaulets, one can only wonder. Sir Edward was never keen on the Navy. Speaking of the son," Papa said in a conspiratorial voice, "I understand the sins of the father have followed him home."

Sophie glanced at her father's drink with a wary eye.

"It must be he is the rightful heir," said Mama, in a vocal stream of thought, "though I'm sure news of Sir Edward taking a second wife did not reach here at all. I would have read about it."

"I've been made to understand," her stout husband insisted, "he had an eye for the ladies of the Caribbean." He gave her a scandalous grin. "Hmm? Ha-ha!"

"Papa," Sophie exclaimed, but she could not stop from smiling.

"Mr. Crestwood, please," said his wife, blinking fast, but her lips curled up with the admonition. "It's indeed a quixotic notion, but if he is the new owner of Pembroke Hall then he is most certainly worthy of it unless there has been some undiscovered intrigue." Mama leaned forward in her seat like one of them might share something to drag her thoughts away from the shadowy figures and dense fogs in her books.

Papa shared his gift for sniffing out news the way a hound tracked down a fox. "He did not need the Navy with his family name, so he must have gone to sea under some other circumstance."

"According to Mrs. Porter," offered the seldom chatty Mrs. Crestwood, "the family's holdings in the Indies were lost years ago. A violent storm or earthquake, or perhaps a horrific fire burned the plantation to the ground. It must have been tragic." She hesitated then looked down at her plate with pity in her eyes.

Papa's conversation frothed along with his wife's encouragement like a tidal wave. "I doubt it was a natural event. It's no secret Sir Edward spent the family fortune on gaming and drink, the poor devil. He always did like to sport, even before he went..."

His voice faltered, and he scowled as if recalling a memory but shook himself out of it the way a horse tossed its head. Sophie looked at her mother who frowned over her half-eaten meal. Papa carried on: "Pembroke's heir must keep up some manner of business in St. Kitts, else he lies heavily in debt."

"Pirating," offered Jack. "He is a captain after all, even if it ain't the Navy."

Mama's head jerked up, and her eyes held a curious light. "No, I could never believe it." She repositioned herself in her chair and picked up her fork. Papa, looking both pleased and aghast, declared, "We shall soon find him out." He stabbed another carrot.

"Poor Captain Murdock," Sophie said, chuckling as she did so. "He's only just arrived and already his title is questioned, his income decided, and his career open to speculation."

"The word is he is no *poor* man, my dear." Papa looked around the table and lowered his voice. "I hear tell he intends to refurbish Pembroke Hall to its original glory. It will take a great deal of money."

"Well, he could not do so on a lieutenant's pay," Jack said.

Papa's smile gleamed in agreement.

"Let us presume he is respectable," Sophie decided. "You should call on him and welcome him home, Papa. Then we shall puzzle it all out."

Her father frowned again and fell silent. In the peculiar quiet, Mama said without looking up, "He must have come into his fortune some other way."

"Buccaneering," Jack repeated, and though Sophie raised her eyes to the aging plaster ceiling, this time neither one of her parents corrected him. Her father looked both excited and appalled, while her mother's expression remained distant.

"When will Richard come again, Papa?" Sophie wondered, to change the direction of their coarse conversation. Her elder brother had been married over a year, and his visits to Leatherbury had been few and far between.

"Lavinia writes they will not be able to return in time for the assembly," said Mama. No one could deny the disappointment in her tone.

"They won't attend?" Sophie grimaced. "I do miss Lavinia. I'd hoped they would stay with us for a time."

"Yes, we need them here," her father harrumphed. "Besides," he nodded at Jack, "we could use an extra man in our fishing party."

Jack glowered at his plate. "Which Richard don't like to fish or hunt," he said, using his vulgar deckhand vernacular. "I'm twice the shot he is."

"Oh, ho!" laughed Papa, "I see a contest in our future."

"He's no match, Papa," Sophie agreed. She leaned across the table. "Jack's quite the marksman and fisherman, too, but Richard is better with accounts." Jack gave her a rueful look.

"It's true," she said with a shrug. "You're as poor at figures as your sister."

"I am not," he said, his ire rising.

"Now, boy," said Papa, for Jack's temper, was as well acknowledged as his sister's candid observations.

"My dear," their mother interrupted, eyeing her son with consolation, "you do not need to be a good shot to be a clergyman. Your living is waiting for you to come of age thanks to Lady Mary. After Oxford, you will get your inheritance and settle at Oak Grove, and there in its elegant parsonage you'll raise a lovely family with a pretty little wife who will be grateful for the situation."

"Which may well be above her own," Papa added. "It's a fine situation for you, Jack."

Sophie bit her lip as their words fluttered through the air and settled across the table like dry leaves. Jack stared down in silent exasperation. Mama's lips were pressed together in a stiff line. Margaret chose that moment to enter with another course.

"Treacle-dowdy," exclaimed Sophie with pretended delight. "I've waited all the day long!"

THE NEXT MORNING SOPHIE went to the library and pulled out the only book of maps at Leatherbury. It did not offer up a great many details, but the islands of the West Indies were carefully drawn and labeled. She wondered where their new neighbor had lived. Antigua? Tortuga, perhaps? Her mind raced. St. Kitts, Papa had said.

Someone had drawn a black flag beside a little dot. Jack, no doubt. Poor boy. Sophie knew her parents believed Jack's dreams of seamanship to be a passing fancy, but he had set his heart on a naval career before he was out of strings.

Sophie let out a heavy breath over the drawings. It was her duty to marry well. Mr. Crestwood was a country gentleman with a generous income, but it had not increased when he won his wife's consent so many years ago. If only he'd been titled. Sophie was certain that was all that was lacking in her favor. Her family was respectable. They had a good living and were settled in her father's ancestral home in Higfield, a stone's toss from Guildford, almost equally between London and Portsmouth. It was a convenient location, but none of it had made her a young bride. She had tried, really, she had and so cheerfully, but—

"Miss Crestwood?"

Sophie looked up from her contemplations. Margaret stood at the door wringing a cloth in her chubby hands. "Mr. Lyman can't find Master Jack."

"That boy!" Sophie slid off the honey-colored sofa and set the book back on its shelf. "I have a good idea where he may be found." She snatched a bonnet and shawl then strode out the back of the house beyond the kitchen garden.

Once through the gate, she forgot her urgency and slowed her pace, skipping across the greening pastures beyond Leatherbury. A silvery light shined over the land like it knew winter had kissed the world goodbye for good.

Sophie strolled through scattered groves of trees until the woods began to thicken. Uncertain of her direction, she stopped for a time and studied the landscape. She tried to recall the direction of the small lake her brother so loved. It was rather a large pond, but the family insisted on calling it a lake. She assumed this was because it sounded grander, but it was only a murky green body of water with some good fish and a few waterfowl.

Looking ahead, the view stopped her in her tracks. It was not the lake, but the crumbling grey peaks of Pembroke in the distance. Sharp, formidable chimneys stood frozen above the hills hinting at some foreboding curse. They were dark and ragged, grasping at the sky with angry fingers as if intent on pulling the heart out of heaven itself. She swallowed and took a step into a pool of light.

The sun warmed the morning pleasantly enough so there was no chill creeping through her layers. In her favorite walking dress and faded spencer, Sophie clambered over the dilapidated stile that bridged a stone wall separating one pasture from another. On one side lived Leatherbury, warm and busy, with happy animals and eager flower buds. On the other side slept Pembroke.

Sophie looked up the hill at the towering manor, trying to imagine life within or without its walls. Pembroke answered like a giant shadow challenging the day. She suspected the foundation was ever more gnarled with weeds and ivy than when she last saw it, holding itself prisoner on its very own property. It seemed forever doomed to crumble away and sink into the earth like a ship into the sea.

The rumbling sound of hoofbeats made Sophie turn her head to look. From out of a copse of trees blocking her view, appeared a rider on a dark bay mount. The gleaming horse slowed to a trot and spying her, its master veered it off toward the echelon of stone and approached her.

Sophie stepped back against the wall, leaning into the cool rocks for support. When he came to a halt within a few paces, the man removed his cocked hat, a black Naval-looking issue with a pretty blue cockade. It stood out, just as his bright eyes stood out against his tanned features. Unlike the neat bicorn, his long and wild hair looked unkempt.

She had imagined the dark silhouette would take the shape of a specter, perhaps with a sickle in its grip; instead, the man appeared to be a gentleman, although not an altogether cheerful looking one. Other than his hat, he was rather too brown and rumpled.

The horse snorted and turned its head to look. The rider studied her, too. Sophie pushed off the wall and stepped forward.

"You are from Leatherbury?" he assumed in a flat tone.

"Miss Crestwood of Leatherbury," she informed him, trying to maintain her poise. Her attempt was foiled by an examining gaze with eyes so pale she could not tell their color. She couldn't look at him without glancing away and back again.

"Then, Miss Crestwood of Leatherbury, I recommend you and your family reacquaint yourselves with the boundaries of your estate."

Her mouth dropped open at the ill-mannered admonition. Sophie stared up at the horseman from beneath the brim of her bonnet, aware she was mussed and the hem of her skirt damp with morning dew. One of her ribbons, frayed at the end, fluttered up in her face, but she did not shoo it away. "I am looking for my brother," she said, trying to gather up enough dismay to feel slighted. "I assure you I am within the boundaries of my home."

The man gazed off into the distance behind her. "I beg your pardon," he said with a slight apologetic cough, "but your boundaries are the low-lying stream several yards beyond the grove, to where I suspect I've just chased your brother from my orchard."

"Please accept my apologies then." Sophie kept her tone stiff.

She whirled away toward the stile to escape his censure, wondering why she did not debate with him that the wall had been the boundary for ages. Everyone knew it, even the cows. She was a Crestwood from Leatherbury, and she knew it. Who was he to tell her differently?

She pivoted back on her heel. "And you are?" She inclined her head and raised her chin, just like Lady Mary did when she questioned some poor, culpable soul.

The man shifted in his saddle like he might slide off the horse, and the animal whinnied and stamped its feet. "Captain Edward Murdock of St. Kitts and still you are trespassing on my property."

Sophie swallowed. Her cheeks flamed with embarrassment. Captain Murdock, Jack's imagined buccaneer, with a look of disapproval on his sun-browned face was anything but gracious. Gathering her skirts, she turned her back on him. She dared not look; she would not be angry or show any offense. He would feel awful, she just knew it, when he realized he'd made a horrible mistake. How cold and cruel and above all rudely suspicious to behave like she was intruding with some wicked scheme in mind. The poor man was misinformed.

A small flash of something round and black flew past her head. She winced, just as the horse snorted in pain. The mount squealed and reared, and Sophie watched in dismay as it forced the captain to cling desperately to the reins to keep from falling off. The look on his set jaw could have lit a match. He called down the beast, but it was no good. Taking a deep breath, she called out, "Welcome to Higfield, Captain Murdock." He was too busy to reply.

Another shot fired from the grove like a miniature cannonball and smashed into the stone wall with a crack. Sophie jerked at the explosive sound and watched the startled horse race back up the pasture hill in the direction it had come. The rider flailed as he struggled to stay astride.

Sophie's hand flew up to her mouth to stifle a laugh. She looked in the direction of the unseen attacker and made a face of furious warning less someone be hurt. Once over the stile, she strode into the woods to find Jack.

He was waiting for her underneath a giant walnut tree, with a grin on his face. "Capital aim, wouldn't you say?"

Sophie could not hide her amusement, but she tried to sound stern. "You could have killed one of us, and you spooked his poor horse!"

"I hit his mount right where I intended."

"What will Papa say," Sophie asked, "when word is sent to Leatherbury? Oh Jack, what trouble you've made for us now. This isn't boarding school. That was Captain Murdock himself." She snatched her brother's arm and forced him to escort her through the trees.

"I was defending my sister."

"Gentlemen don't hide behind trees and lob nuts. Really, Jack, if he is truly angry he might call you out."

"Me?" Jack spread his hands out in an innocent gesture. "I'm just a lad."

"No, you are a young man, and it's time you start acting the part. If you want to convince the family you are fit for a naval career you must quit running through the forest like Robin Hood."

"Mama did mention the army," Jack reminded her. "I am going to sea, but at least she's opened her mind to something other than a cassock." He led his worried sister by the hand through a maze of young saplings and tangled briars that would soon droop with fat berries.

"Leatherbury is this way, Sophie. You've no direction at all. At least look up and follow the sun."

"I have good sense, of which you have none. We best hurry and get you back to Mr. Lyman before he tells Papa."

"I'm sure he won't notice."

"He has noticed, and he's sent Margaret to find you. They've probably alerted the entire household, and now we will run into Old George if we're not careful."

"That old fool? I'm twice the gamekeeper he is."

"Just because he's losing his sight doesn't mean he can't track down the likes of you."

Jack shook his head in disagreement. "I've been dodging Old George for years now. It's the pirate next door that's the problem."

"You can't say he's a pirate, Jack. It's a vicious lie."

"Did you see the dagger at his side?"

Sophie nodded.

"Gold, covered in jewels, and glimmering in the sunlight." Jack lost himself in a slow, pensive daydream.

"You are such a romantic, silly boy. He's probably uneasy about poachers since he's just arrived. Pembroke's been deserted for years."

"I'm not romantic, Sophie. The fellow ain't been here a week, and already he guards his estate like a bull."

"Perhaps he was riding out to get a feel for it."

"He already knows the boundaries," Jack insisted.

"Yes, it's true." Sophie reflected on Captain Murdock's confident knowledge of the stream bed she had maneuvered around and then the stone wall. "I imagine he's studied Pembroke's papers."

"You mean maps. All pirates can read maps." Jack eyed her with gravity.

Sophie gave him a teasing smile back. "You sound like Mama. She was reading that *Robinson Crusoe* this morning."

"I read it ages ago."

"Then I suppose you must know everything about which you assume: Captain Murdock is indeed a pirate, the stone wall is the estate's boundaries, and you are well on your way to an infamous naval career."

Affronted, Jack let go of her arm and darted toward Leatherbury. It had come into view in the distance.

"Jack!" Sophie cried with exasperation, but he did not look back. Huffing in the warm air and put out with wandering boys and boundaries, she marched back home and up to her room to change her dirty gown and not think about Captain Edward Murdock of St. Kitts...

Purchase A Pirate at Pembroke online or at book-stores today!

ABOUT THE AUTHOR

Danielle Thorne is the author of classic romance and adventure in several genres. She loves Jane Austen, pirates, beaches, cookies, antiques, cats, dogs, and long naps. She does not like phone calls or sushi. A graduate of BYU-Idaho, Danielle saw early work published by *Arts and Prose Magazine, Mississippi Crow, The Nantahala Review, StorySouth,* and – you get the idea. Besides writing, she's edited for both Solstice and Desert Breeze Publishing. During free time, which means when Netflix is down, she combs through feedback on her novels and offers virtual hugs for reviews. Her next adventure is coming soon.

Visit the author at www.daniellethorne.com
Twitter: @DanielleThorne
Facebook: Author Danielle Thorne
Instagram: authordaniellethorne

OTHER BOOKS BY DANIELLE THORNE

The Privateer
Josette
A Pirate at Pembroke
By Heart and Compass
Turtle Soup
Valentine Gold
Henry's Holiday Charade
Death Cheater
Cheated
Southern Girl, Yankee Roots
Garland's Christmas Romance
A Smuggler's Heart (Spring 2020)
His Daughter's Prayer (Summer 2020)

Made in the USA
Coppell, TX
29 January 2020

15147173R00120